GUNFIRE AT ARGON

GUNFIRE AT ARGON

Gates had moved on to land near the town of Argon to live his life in peace, but two events disturbed that peace. His friend, the Argon lawman, died and a boy named Orford assumed the post. Then Quint and his roughnecks set up the robbery of the Argon Bank and Loan. Against his will, Gates was drawn into the ensuing stand-off. A bitter, dangerous gunbattle erupted and at the end of it, Argon was never to be the same again.

GUNFIRE
AT ARGON

by
Lee F. Gregson

Dales Large Print Books
Long Preston, North Yorkshire,
England.

British Library Cataloguing in Publication Data.

Gregson, Lee F.
Gunfire at Argon.

A catalogue record for this book is
available from the British Library

ISBN 1-85389-696-9 pbk

First published in Great Britain by Robert Hale Ltd., 1995

Copyright © 1995 by Lee F. Gregson

The right of Lee F. Gregson to be identified as the author
of this work has been asserted by him in accordance with
the Copyright, Designs and Patents Act, 1988

Published in Large Print December, 1996 by arrangement
with Robert Hale Ltd.

Dales Large Print is an imprint of
Library Magna Books Ltd.
Printed and bound in Great Britain by
T.J. Press (Padstow) Ltd., Cornwall, PL28 8RW.

ONE

Sunlight was dappled across the bare, stained floor of the Argon sheriff's office, papers were piled on the old wooden desk, but there was no sign whatsoever of Restall himself.

The big man, Gates, walked on through the office into the narrow passageway where the single, barred cell was, observing that it was empty apart from a slop-bucket, and smelled of a disinfectant strong enough to overpower all other odours: and passing beyond the passageway, he entered by another doorway the spartan living-quarters at the back of the building.

'George?' He heard, he thought, a faint response, so moved on to the room that he knew was where Restall slept, and sure enough found him there. The Argon sheriff was lying fully dressed on top of a narrow cot, his face sunken and slick with

7

sweat, his breathing laboured and sounding liquid.

'Who's that?' Restall's voice was scarcely audible, and after he spoke he began coughing in a bubbly way that, when the spasm was over, left him gasping, his breath wheezing.

'George, I'll go fetch the doc.'

One limp, bony-wristed hand was raised, then fell back. 'No...cain't do nothin'.' Gates' offer had been little more than a reaction to his sighting of George Restall, for he knew already that what the prone man had said was perfectly true. 'Ain't got long,' Restall said. 'Not now.'

Gates, though, was moved to persist, such was Restall's condition.

'Somebody needs to be here. I'll shut the office an' then I'll go fetch Bess Lanyon.' Before he turned away though, Gates asked, 'Where's Matt Orford?'

Restall's wheezy breathing continued for a spell, as though further talk was beyond him, but then he said, 'Ain't showed up yet.'

'I'll go get Bess.' When Restall made

no response Gates read it as a kind of exhausted acquiescence and went back along the passage and into the office and once there he shut the street door and slid the bolts, then again walked through the building and let himself out the back way.

The Lanyon house was a couple of streets away, and Bess, glancing from her kitchen window as he went along the walk beside the house, showed concern on her plump face and at once appeared on the porch, drying her reddened hands on her apron, and intuitively she knew what it must be that had brought Gates here at this time of day.

'It's Mr Restall, isn't it?'

He nodded. 'George doesn't look too good at all; an' he won't have the doc.'

'I'll go over right away.'

Gates did not go any further, knowing that Bob Lanyon, the wheelwright, would be busy in his workshop out back; the son, Jay, would be at the bank where he worked; and of more interest to Gates, the Lanyons' niece, Stella Freeman, would be teaching her classes up at the Argon schoolhouse. As he was turning away, though, Bess said; 'We've not seen much of you of late, Dave.' He assumed that she meant that Stella hadn't.

'I know, Bess; but I'll drop by soon.' Another faint voice in his head warned him that it might not be so, perhaps should not be so.

'See you do.' She went down the walk, intent now on finding out what she could do for George Restall's comfort, which, Gates considered, with all her great goodwill, would not be very much for she knew as well as he did and as did the old man himself, that Restall was dying and that at this stage nothing could be done by anybody to reverse that process. It had been merely a question of time, and now that time was almost up.

Gates, going about his own affairs once again, visited a couple of suppliers; then, moving at an easy pace, walked along Main to where his small, flat-deck wagon stood, some supplies already stacked on it, the docile, ear-flicking mare standing between the shafts.

A tall, muscular, narrow-hipped man with a leathery skin, he might have been touching forty, yet there was a certain litheness to him, and his slate-dark eyes, their corners fanned with wrinkles, were still the eyes of hazy distances, often devoid of readable expression, but nonetheless alert. A taciturn man, Gates, who a year and a half ago had bought some land and a homestead not far out of Argon; a man who had made few friends, who had kept much to himself, who went unarmed, yet who had stirred no little amount of speculation. And he knew that there were men in Argon who would have been just as pleased to see him sell up and move on, for no better reason than that at times there was something unsettling about him, about the way he moved and looked.

About to step up and untie the reins, he turned as a man in a tweed suit and a derby hat spoke to him, and he nodded as the attorney, Charles Redwine, approached.

'A few minutes ago,' Redwine said, 'I spoke with Mrs Lanyon' (he broke off to raise his hat to some people, passing) 'and she tells me that George Restall is very bad right now.'

'Yeah,' said Gates, 'I think it's about all up for old George. Bess Lanyon will do what she can: clean him up, make meals if he can still eat. He wouldn't let me fetch Doc Brill.'

'And Orford? Where's Matt Orford?'

'Not around the office, anyway. George didn't know where he was.'

'The boy is simply not up to it, not responsible enough,' Redwine said of the deputy.

'Well,' said Gates, his slate eyes unreadable, 'it's likely he'll soon be the only peace officer you've got.'

'May the good Lord forbid,' Redwine said feelingly. For a moment Gates glanced away at people criss-crossing Main, well knowing what Redwine was thinking but not wishing to get into that particular discussion. He put a boot on the wagon-step and got up on the seat. 'And you know what my own views happen to be,' Redwine said.

'Yeah, I do know, but if you're anglin' around to another question, you know what my views are, an' the answer would be the same as it was the last time,' Gates said.

From pouchy eyes Redwine stood studying the man up on the wagon but said no more on that subject, for as far as Gates was concerned he had learned to go just so far and no further. There were matters either known about or suspected by Redwine that even in drink, as frequently he was, he would stop short of broaching with this man, things that he kept strictly to himself. Sometimes he had come to wonder if Gates possessed more than ordinary powers for there had been moments, whenever they had talked, when these same slate eyes had seemed suddenly to probe more deeply, as though they were capable of reading what was going through the attorney's mind.

About to release the brake, Gates got as far as putting his hand on the lever but paused when a big, hard-faced man came pacing towards them, Redwine turning his head, a faint, rather sardonic smile on his lips.

At first glance Ranse Jago was impressive in his eastern-suit and stiff-brimmed hat, but at the next, seemed somewhat incongruously dressed in such smart attire because of his leathery outdoor ruggedness; like a man who had strayed out of his natural milieu. And that indeed was what had happened. A man who had forsaken the cattle business for more sedentary pursuits, was Jago; and though oftentimes trailed by one or another of the men from his saloon or his lumber business, right now he was on his own.

A yard short of Redwine he came to a stop, lighting a fat cigar, then flicking the smoke-trailing match into the street.

'Well now,' said Jago, 'the attorney an' the sodbuster, no less. So which one's consultin' which?'

'What you see is nothing more than a private conversation,' Redwine said mildly.

'Now there's another thing,' Jago said in his hard, penetrating voice. 'Takin' into account the time o' day, an' here we are, attorney, still near to sober.' Redwine's face tautened at the jibe but he merely stared silently at Jago, refusing to be provoked. Anyway, if it should turn nasty he would be no physical match for this man and he well knew it. When Jago half turned his head to stare at the man on the wagon, the deep dislike was plain enough to see. 'An' the man that come from nowhere,' Jago said, 'a nobody from nowhere. Yuh come in to sell beans, mister?'

'No point,' said Gates evenly, 'in tryin' to sell beans to them that's got more than enough gas already. Like Redwine told you, it's a private conversation.' He was aware that Redwine's eyes were fixed on him now with a strange expression that lay somewhere between eagerness and trepidation.

'There's but one thing that's worse than a sodbuster,' Jago said, 'an' that's a sodbuster with a sassy mouth. It'll earn yuh some problems yuh can't handle afore too much longer, mister.'

This time Gates did not answer him but released the wagon-brake, nodded to the tense Redwine and flicked the reins, the mare walking stolidly away, Jago's malevolent eyes following him. Gates was very well aware that the man's unprovoked enmity towards him had less to do with the fact that he was a farmer and rather more to do with the friendly familiarity he found at the Lanyon household where Stella Freeman lived.

Holding the mare down to a gentle walk, Gates carried on up Main, not looking back, though he did cast one glance up towards the small schoolhouse, but there was no sign of life there. But heading out of town along a well-defined trail he saw a lone horseman ambling towards him and hauled the wagon to a halt as Matt Orford, Restall's deputy, pulled alongside.

The bony young man, his prominent Adam's apple working, passed the time of day, grinning amiably until Gates told him about Restall. Gates did not enquire as to where Orford had been, for it was none of his business, but he did say, 'If you want to be of any help to George, now's the time.'

'He's gonna die, ain't he?' The young man's eyes were wide with apparent concern, but something else was there—almost, Gates thought, a hunger. *That would leave just me. If Restall cashes in, it would leave me.*

'Yeah, I'd say George is more than halfway to a box,' Gates said, 'so you'd best get down there. Bess Lanyon's with him.' He clicked his tongue, flicked the reins and walked the mare on again.

Parting from Orford, Gates was left to his own brooding thoughts. Seeing the young man with the deputy's badge on his vest, reading what, for a moment, Orford had been unable to conceal, had fetched a few of Gates' demons from out of the shadows, ruffled memories better left to lie undisturbed, and it had been like a quick, chill wind from the past.

As he drove along in the sometimes swaying, constantly creaking, wagon, his sombre mood deepened and the more his thoughts went ranging over the past and lingered over newly-perceived links with the present, the more did he come to feel that he would have been pleased to have been driving out of Argon for good. Coming to this part of the country, all he had wished for was to make a peaceful place for himself where perhaps he might even see out the rest of his days. Now he was beginning to have doubts that such a fancy would ever become a reality, though certainly not because he had sought quarrels. On the contrary, the doubts he was feeling now had roots in quite other human contacts; they were arising because of acquaintanceships that had begun, some of them anyway, to develop into friendships—Redwine, Restall, the Lanyons, Stella Freeman—which in turn had begun to attract the interest of others, and in the case of Ranse Jago, scarcely concealed enmity. Perhaps it had been a lesson that up to now he had not really learned; that a man, no matter what his motivations, could not truly choose to be a man alone, and succeed. And now the growing evidence of this lesson had brought with it an unsettling premonition of trouble, all woven into, somewhat confusingly, the last days of a dying man. It was with some irritation that he flicked the reins, waking the mare up rudely, increasing her stride, anxious now to distance himself from Argon.

TWO

It went all to hell in an unlikely dump called Meer's Crossing.

Quint himself, Sears, Pearsall and Reeby, pistols drawn, had gone into the bank; and because there were six horses in all, both Hall and Mavor had stayed back to watch out for them, both sitting up on their own mounts while also surveying the length of the street and muttering about the nuisance of blown dust and watching the wind-blown tumbleweeds coming bowling along. And the people who happened to be abroad at the time saw what was happening up at the bank and started running for cover.

Up to that point the bank had looked none too difficult a proposition and perhaps because of that and the fact that there were six of them and they had come in, as Quint was to observe later, on the blind, they were caught wrong-footed from the start. For what Quint did not know was that, having paused overnight in Meer's Crossing, having bunked down in the long barn behind the livery, and now having completed their ablutions and eaten breakfast, a small detachment of the U.S. Cavalry—a corporal and four troopers—was at this moment mounted up and about to come out onto Main. Just before they emerged, however, they must also have been made aware of what was taking place up there at the bank, for now the corporal prudently halted them, dismounted them as for a skirmish-line, and they made a much more circumspect appearance (one trooper detailed to watch over their horses) to get a quiet look for themselves.

As soon as he saw the first two soldiers Mavor began shouting a warning and

Hall was even more positive, letting go a rocketing shot, causing the troopers—now three of them—to spread out and the Quint horses to begin moving around in alarm, jerking their heads up.

That sure did sweep the streets clean of the remnants of the foolish and the curious. Then Mavor, unpredictable as always, yelled for Hall to take charge of the Quint horses and pulled his own mount away, hauling it sideways into the middle of the street, blasting in the direction of the blue-clad soldiers; and in an ill-advised move, even made a jerky approach on his unsettled horse, shouting and firing. And that was when one of the troopers, going to one knee, hunched over, lined up a carbine and banged one away at Mavor and hit him, first jolting him up and back in the saddle before he went over sideways just as the horse panicked in full measure and began galloping along the street towards the cavalrymen. Mavor, out of the saddle but with a boot still caught up in the stirrup, was being jerked savagely and buffeted, now screaming, coming through the raking dust, still clinging as though for life itself to the heavy pistol. When the badly spooked horse got to where the troopers' line was, one of them jumped up and began running alongside Mavor, and ignoring his wide, imploring eyes, put a pistol to Mavor's head and shot him, so that the terrified horse, running on, was now dragging with it a flopping, blood-spattering dead man. The trooper slowed down and turned and came jogging back to his position, the corporal crouching nearby in a doorway, shouting further orders.

By now Quint, Sears, Pearsall—Pearsall boldly distinguishable in a long, buff-coloured coat—and Reeby had come bursting one after another out of the bank to see Hall in trouble, losing control of the animals, which were scattering; and Quint, his eyes staring wide, began bawling, 'Jesus! Git them goddamn' broncs caught up!'

Hall, still mounted, with Sears and Reeby afoot, running, immediately went out to try to do it, for without these horses, nobody was going anywhere, except maybe to hell. The men afoot were ducking as low as they could as they ran, for the gunfire now coming from the troopers was increasing and it was not long before Sears yelped and went down on one knee, clutching at his left side.

Quint and the long-coated Pearsall were now both down on one knee out in the street and had begun firing with calm deliberation, and when one of the soldiers who had a carbine stood up, the long stock of it to his shoulder, Quint hit him fair and square with a clean pistol-shot, a real good long-shot that set the others there ducking for cover, leaving the shot trooper sitting in the street, his cap gone, looking up towards Quint and Pearsall with a dazed expression on his face, dying.

Dust was rising only to be immediately plucked away by the wind as Hall, still in the saddle, and Reeby and Sears, working feverishly, began imposing order among the jittery loose horses. And they were beginning to get the animals pretty much under control when, with a sound like a wet cloth slapping bare flesh, Hall was hit by a .45 from one of the carbines and punched from the saddle to roll slackly among the tumbleweeds and lie still, sightless eyes staring at the sky.

Now Pearsall, bending low, ran across to help with the horses while Quint, with a fine disregard for the lethal, whipping lead, even went a few paces up Main, still shooting in a measured way; but he could now perceive that if they should all try to mount out in the open, they would make of themselves prime targets for the carbines.

'Hitch 'em an' take cover!' Quint roared, thinking that they were not going to get the horses hauled back across Main, and took himself up onto the boardwalk.

Sporadic shouting now ensued among the military, and by this time Oakes, the Meer's Crossing sheriff, had arrived and joined the soldiers, and ruddy-faced, white whiskers bristling, was also blasting shots spiritedly along Main.

Pearsall now took the initiative, and calling to Reeby managed to get all the horses in hand and on the move, and under this comparative control went jogging with them around the corner of the bank building. And when he saw what they were achieving, the injured Sears, blood on the left side of his shirt, went awkwardly after them, while the long-coated Pearsall, now having taken a shotgun off his own horse, yelled for Quint to come on back while he covered him. So Quint came backing along the boardwalk trying to reload the pistol and watch what the troopers were up to as well, Pearsall letting go a thumping blast with the shotgun, and then another, to put all the skirmishers' heads down fast, for even though the range was considerable the discharge of a shotgun had had a predictable effect.

Once around the corner, Quint said, 'Let's git shot o' this fly-trap.' And then, 'Is Hall done for?'

'Yeah, shot clean,' Reeby said.

Having calmly discarded the spent cartridges and inserted fresh loads in his shotgun, Pearsall fired again; then half turning, he let rip the other barrel straight at the bank, to blow the single, painted window in with a fearful, glass-bursting racket. He then went ducking around the corner.

They swung up, leaving Hall's horse where it was, and went out and across the end of Main at a gathering run, a strange silence behind them; though not because the troopers had given up, nor the lawman, Oakes, but because they, too, were busy climbing into saddles, Oakes taking the dead trooper's mount and all bent on running the bastards down if it was the last thing they would ever do.

Quint, Pearsall, Reeby and the drawn-faced, injured Sears lost no time in departing from the well-defined trail out of Meer's Crossing and heading into the brushy uplands which soon gave way to parched and broken country that was seen to be running towards a series of sharp ridges rising against the sky. When they had ridden with some urgency for almost half an hour, Quint called out and they began to slow the labouring horses, at last easing right back and finally coming to a halt, the three who had been ahead now waiting for Sears to come up with them.

Quint, his teak-like face whitened like the faces of the others, with dust clinging to the sweat on it, the thongs of his shallow-crowned, greasy hat hanging loose as he wiped at face and forehead with a sleeve, dismounted and made his way across to an upthrust of reddish rock. Taking care where he was putting his boots, his chest still heaving from the hard ride, Quint managed to work his way up until he was at an elevation of about twenty-five feet, and once there he took a good look at all the bad country they had just passed through.

At this stage Pearsall took off his long coat, and first removing some shotgun cartridges from one of the pockets, bundled it up and tied it with his bedroll behind the cantle. Reeby gave Sears a hand to get down out of the saddle and Sears immediately sank down to sit on the ground. Reeby looked at him then unshipped his own canteen and soaked a bandanna and when Sears eased his shirt up and sat there with breath hissing through his teeth, Reeby did what he could to clean the wound.

'Went clear through,' he muttered, observing the very ugly, blood-suppurating welt across Sears' side above the hip-bone, a wound that had led to considerable loss of blood which had by this time made an unsightly mess down the left leg of Sears' pants. Reeby wrung out the bandanna, then fashioned it into a long pad and wadded it against the length of the wound and Sears then gingerly drew his shirt down over it.

Pearsall, his dead eyes watching Quint who was now carefully descending the rock, asked, 'They comin'?'

Quint jumped down the last four feet, staggered forward, swore sharply, then recovered. 'Yeah, seen their goddamn' dust.'

'Well,' Reeby said, looking up, 'what now?'

'One thing I ain't about to do,' said Quint, 'is run these here animals into the ground. We cain't afford that. No, we'll wait, boys, and we'll suck these shits in.'

'Carbines,' muttered Reeby almost to himself. Sears had no need to say anything. He knew all about carbines.

'We'll pick the place,' said Quint.

And so it transpired. First, though, they sought out a particular feature of the land, a passage between rearing rocks, before they set about creating some quite visible dust of their own; then three of them took up concealed positions as Quint directed, Sears being established a little distance away in a place well out of sight, to look after the horses. Pearsall had again taken down his double-barrelled shotgun and there they all waited, knowing that if it went wrong it would likely go badly wrong, and so fast you wouldn't want to know about it.

Downwind of the pursuing riders, they had no difficulty in hearing them coming, but it seemed a long time before they actually came into view; then suddenly there they were, coming fairly quickly, one trooper out in the lead, raising a line of dust all on his own, then the others, looming through it, the angry corporal,

Oakes the Meer's Crossing peacekeeper, then the other two surviving troopers.

Quint permitted the leading rider to come within nearly forty feet before he let go three walloping shots from the long pistol, two of which hit the horse, the other the rider, the horse screaming and knuckling over, hurling the hard-riding trooper from the saddle to go rolling wildly in a welter of arms and legs.

The riders following him were cast instantly into confusion, the corporal yelling at them to go on, some already hesitating, slowing, until finally the corporal, Oakes and one trooper kept riding on, desperately urging their horses to greater effort; but the last trooper had managed to slow down and then stop and was now trying to get the horse turned around to go back whence he had come. Then Pearsall stood up, his shotgun thumping once, spewing smoke and wads, and close enough for the still-bunched shot to whack solidly into the soldier's upper body and knock him clean out of the saddle to bounce and flop over in a bloodied mass in the moving dust.

Quint and Reeby, some twenty feet above the horsemen, were firing their pistols through this dust, and Reeby suddenly shouted exultantly, 'I got one! I got one o' the bastards!' And when some of the dust went drifting away on the breeze, sure enough a riderless horse, reins flying, was galloping in the wake of the ridden horses and the man who was down was hopelessly trying to crawl away. Quint himself went scrambling down out of the big rocks, and within the space of half a minute he was running in awkwardly on his high-heeled boots, but really had plenty of time to get to the now hatless trooper—for indeed this was the last of the corporal's section—and blow the top of his head off.

Meanwhile, coming clear of that lethal rocky pass the survivors, Oakes and the corporal himself, at once split up, Oakes heading left, the corporal right, whether simply to confuse the ambushers or by some spontaneous mutual agreement to effect some kind of encircling movement, was unclear. In the event it turned out to be a whole heap of bad luck for the corporal to add to the bad luck he had already had that day, for in one moment he was free and clear, making his rapid sweep around to the right, mercifully beyond the sight now of those who had caused such unimaginable havoc among his troopers, when all at once he found himself almost on top of a bunch of horses; and not only that, but there was a man with them, and it would be debatable whether or not the corporal actually heard the thunderclap of Sears' pistol, for the big slug took him in the left eye, bowling him off the running horse, flinging him down among the hooves of the picketed mounts, setting them tugging wildly and wheeling and snorting in alarm.

The dust was still moving like a whitish veil above the scene of the main action as Pearsall with his shotgun and Quint and Reeby came tramping around to where Sears was, now sitting again, looking very tired, still holding the big Colt.

Reeby wondered aloud where the other one had gone.

'If he's got any goddamn' sense,' Quint said, 'he's quirtin' that animal all the way back to his shit-heap town.' Which might very well have been the case, for they saw not even a whisker after that of the Meer's Crossing lawman.

It gave them enough confidence, anyway, to move on only another mile or so before making a camp, mainly so that Sears could rest up and the horses could be spelled; and it gave Quint a chance to get his thoughts together, which he did, once he had finished cussing.

They had got away with it, just, for it could easily have gone the other way; and having lost Hall and Mavor, having had to abandon the proceeds from the bank—poor as they had been—back there on that street, now they had got a wounded man to drag along as well. For Sears had lost a lot of blood and clearly would not be able to stand up to a long ride for a good long while, so there was a pressing need for them to give a lot of thought about what to do next.

'One thing,' Quint said, 'we'll never make that mistake again. Never. We'll never go in on the blind.'

THREE

So now old George Restall was dead and his burial was over, and Matt Orford, no longer difficult to locate, was quite demonstrably having some difficulty in treading that fine, if unseen, line that lay between due deference in the presence of recent death and the barely-suppressed anticipation of new personal powers.

The youthful deputy was perhaps mercifully unaware that this palpably eager assumption of such new powers had been the subject of discussion even while Restall had still been alive, though in serious decline, among those who were reckoned to be the most influential citizens of Argon. After all, it had become perfectly obvious to everybody that this moment must soon arrive, but of course until it did the awkward reality did not need to be confronted. A number of factors, however, now arose for consideration before any decision could be made. There was the unarguable fact of Matt Orford's youth, his pronounced brashness, his known propensity for riding the badge in situations where arguably a more conciliatory approach might be called for. And now old Restall would no longer be around to counsel him and, if necessary, rein him in. Consequently a certain widely felt if up to now largely unexpressed nervousness had begun to surface among some of the townspeople; and there were speculations of a more worldly nature among others.

When Ranse Jago, standing on the fringe of the now slowly dispersing crowd, cigar between his teeth, half turned his large head, there within his view was Orford, skinny in his levis and blue denim shirt and black string tie, pacing around, talking endlessly, moving among those who for a variety of reasons had turned out for the burial of the old sheriff, shaking selected hands, acting more in the nature of some busily-campaigning politician than of a deputy sheriff of limited experience who had just seen the town's senior and respected peacekeeper lowered into the dusty earth.

Gates' slate eyes, too, picked out particular faces from among the slowly-moving people and the lingering groups, seeing Jago there ruminatively drawing on his cigar and now speculatively studying the garrulous deputy. And there were two of Jago's men, one named Culp, the other Mellish, hard-eyed, prowling the fringes of the gathering, glancing frequently in Jago's direction, perhaps waiting for a nod or a gesture of dismissal. And the Lanyons were there, Robert and Bess and their son, Jay, who worked at the bank, all turned out in their neat, if slightly rubbed, Sunday clothes; and the coolly good-looking niece, Stella Freeman, who once or twice during this odd hiatus had caught Gates' eye.

Others were noticed by Gates; the

acerbic, narrow-faced Doctor Brill with his pure white hair and eyebrows, a man denied by the now dead Restall; and the derby-hatted, sardonic attorney, Redwine; James Fleury, the pale, fussy senior clerk at the Argon Bank and Loan, his small round eyeglasses glinting, hovering near his employer, the banker, Brophy, who was a tubby little man with quick, appraising brown eyes; a man named Pauling and another Ed Moore, staid shopkeepers both; and considered to be influential men in this town, standing with their straight-lipped wives, examining critically everybody else within sight. Gates knew full well that they, and others, sometimes talked about him, wondered about him, probably passed some sort of judgement on him.

Stella Freeman's large, deep mauve eyes also regarded, but with a calm reservation, many of those others who had come out today to bury Restall, but she had smiled faintly when she had caught Gates' friendly glance and had done her best to avoid Jago's eye when he had been looking towards her with unconcealed interest.

Groups dispersed, reformed elsewhere. The town had virtually closed down for the funeral, and it seemed, now that daily routines had been broken, there was no particular hurry to leave.

Redwine, soft-voiced, studiously courteous, at one point joined the banker, Brophy, who was standing now with Pauling and Moore, freed temporarily from their powder-scented wives, and raised the matter that he thought was probably on more than just his own mind.

'In your view, gentlemen, what ought now to be done about Restall's successor? A direct appointment? An election?' He knew that for some while these particular men had been looking rather askance at Matt Orford; but there were several aspects to be considered, as Redwine well knew.

Moore, a middle-sized, pouch-eyed man, seldom seen to smile, upon hearing the words *direct appointment* shook his head and said again what he had been saying privately to Pauling all through the days of

Restall's decline: 'I for one don't see this young feller Orford as being up to the job. That's my considered opinion.' A strange echo of Redwine's own, as given recently to Gates.

Pauling, scrawny and angular, well enough attired yet never managing to escape a look almost of seediness no matter what he happened to be wearing, stood nodding gently like some tall weed touched by a breeze, but he said nothing. A locally renowned sitter-on-fences, was Pauling.

Brophy, in his small roundness almost nondescript, yet shrewder than either of the shop-keepers by a long shot, took out a slim cigar and after he had lit it, the pleasant-smelling smoke wafting around them all, said what Redwine had expected him to say and what, indeed, would already be in the minds of the other two, no matter what Moore's expressedly considered opinion had been.

'It strikes me that we need do nothing just yet. My first impulse is simply to allow young Orford there to take up the reins, but only on a trial basis. If it should turn out that he's up to it, fine; but if, as you contend, Moore, he isn't, it will show up soon enough and we can look at the matter again.'

What he really meant, so Redwine believed, was that there would be, at least in the short term, substantial savings to be made for the town by having to pay out only one wage for the office of peacekeeping, even if they, as the influential men here, were to cause Orford's money to be marginally increased, even though he would be only on trial in Restall's old job. But it had tended to sound a lot better the way Brophy had chosen to put it, not overtly touching upon this question of money.

Unexpectedly, however, Pauling now cleared his throat. 'You're saying that there won't be any deputy?'

'If a deputy should become necessary in, er, certain circumstances, then Orford could swear in a temporary one,' Brophy said smoothly and glanced at Redwine as though seeking support. 'Couldn't he, counsellor?'

'Oh, indeed he could,' Redwine had to say. But at this point he took a chance—no matter what the man himself might have had to say about it—that he had been quietly waiting for, simply to test the waters of wider opinion, as he added, 'In my humble view, gentlemen, the one who would most naturally assume Restall's duties, of all the men available around Argon, is that man standing over there.'

'Over where?'

Redwine made a small gesture with one hand.

'Gates, you mean?'

'Yes, Dave Gates.'

At first there was a taut silence. Brophy, removing the cigar from his mouth, exhaling a cloud of bluish smoke, was the first to speak up, and to be dismissive. 'Gates? Gates is a...a farmer, Redwine. And he's a recluse. My observations tell me that for some reason Gates almost curls his lip at this town, as though he despises it.

Besides, we know nothing *of* the man, where exactly he came from, why he chose to buy land near Argon in the first place, why he chose to live alone as he does. We know nothing.' Brophy was quite aware, however, that there was an easy friendship between Redwine and Gates.

'But hardly a recluse,' Redwine said mildly.

'What on earth makes you raise Gates' name?' Moore asked, squinting slightly at Redwine as though he had only just noticed that he was there.

Redwine shrugged. 'I don't know for sure, except that he's somewhat older than Matt Orford; and there's a no-nonsense style to the man. I doubt that he'd be the kind to be easily rattled, and in my view he would leave no doubt in anybody else's mind about who was in charge, which, presumably, would be an attribute in a peacekeeper.' He wondered if the banker might be attracted to that notion, for Brophy was himself a man widely known to play the martinet, James

Fleury in particular being said to bear the brunt; which in turn caused Fleury to hand it on down, often to Jay Lanyon.

Pauling then said, 'I reckon Gates wouldn't be the kind to have any interest in a job like that. Anyway, he'd not be at all suitable.' Clearly, for some reason—or for no reason at all—he did not like Gates, though it was quite probable that he had spoken no more than two dozen words to the man since Gates had first appeared in the region.

Redwine did not seek to press the matter for he had recognized at once the wall of opposition to the idea he had floated and, touching the brim of his derby, quietly moved on.

When he had passed out of earshot Brophy remarked that, considering the time of day, he had been astounded that Redwine had not smelled of drink.

Somebody must have allowed the word to get out without wasting any time over it, for a little later, after most of the people had gone home and some businesses had even reopened, Redwine, coming down the external stairs from his office above a saddlery, encountered Jago.

'Don't be in such a goddamn' hurry, mister,' Jago said in his heavy voice. 'What's this I hear about you puttin' this damn' Gates' name up fer peacekeeper?'

Redwine said, 'You're misinformed, Mr Jago. I haven't put anybody's name up. That would need a town meeting. No, I merely mentioned it casually to certain people as a possibility.' Inwardly he cursed Brophy or whoever it had been that had bruited the matter abroad as a formal proposal as soon as his back had been turned.

'Well,' said Jago, 'if it was one o' your better ideas, I don't think much of it. This here town would never sit still fer that sodbuster walkin' the streets. An' anyway, there's somethin' stinks about that feller an' whatever it is will come out sooner or later. So my advice, Redwine, is to forget Gates an' jes' git on with what it is yuh do.'

'It was no more than an expression of

opinion,' Redwine said, flushing slightly under Jago's greeny-eyed stare, 'one that was offered in passing, nothing more than that. Gates himself didn't even know of it.'

'Then it's an opinion,' said Jago, 'that's best buried, like ol' George Restall. Anyway, from what I hear we got oursel's a sheriff already.'

So, thought Redwine, permitted now to move on by, they had talked with Orford already. Heavy-hearted, a familiar depression invading him as he walked on, he decided that the next thing he needed was a drink.

Suddenly despondent, for reasons he could not easily get to grips with, and seeing Stella Freeman in earnest conversation with other people, moving quietly away, principally to avoid the ridiculous, strutting Orford, Gates had slipped alone to his wagon and soon headed home. Restall had become an undemanding friend and would be missed by Gates, and somewhat cynically he wondered just how many among those who had come to pay what they would refer to as *last respects* had had much more interest in the event than that of seizing an opportunity to get dressed up, to see and to be seen, no matter how much Restall had been respected in Argon. To Gates, in the end, it had all seemed to suggest to him that his earlier instincts had been sound, that the best possible policy would be to hold himself aloof, to avoid becoming involved in any of the affairs of the town. On more than one occasion, that had been what he had been trying to convey to Redwine, who seemed to be devising a role for him in the business of that place; and Gates did not want it. Redwine. Gates thought about that studious, rather strange individual, nobody's fool, a man, you would have to say, who was really too good for a dump like Argon, substantial and busy though it was. You could not measure worth by size. Yet there was the matter of Redwine's drinking. That demeaned the man, Gates thought, devalued him. But there had been occasions, true, fleeting moments only, when Gates could almost have sworn that Redwine, sober, *knew* something; that somewhere, somehow, he had discovered matters that belonged in Gates' past, but had held back from broaching them.

These were the thoughts that might well have been the springboard for the uneasy sleep that was awaiting him that night, a sleep peopled with faces that were now unwelcome, recollections of places he had fought to forget, under the faint calling of voices, some of which ought to have been stilled forever.

'Garvey's down! Go left! Go left, the barn's cleared!' Going through curling smoke, near the thunderclaps of the guns, sweating, hurting, eyes dazzled by the lowering, orange sun, going with the urgency of fear, horses squealing somewhere nearby.

Abruptly his eyes sprang open and he found that his body was damp with sweat and there was a nagging sense that he had just passed through some shadow-world filled with menace; but now, in consciousness, it was unreachable in recall.

47

FOUR

Reeby had come across a few clapped-out towns in his time but by his recollection none had been less impressive than Minta, in one of whose two dubious saloons he had just sunk a couple in an attempt to lay the dust. It was late in the day and Reeby was now tired and out of sorts, for he could not for the life of him understand why Quint seemed to have fastened his mind on hitting the bank in a place such as this, even for the sake of trying out what he had explained was a very different approach, and even though, to support what he had said, he had repeated his words uttered in the aftermath of Meer's Crossing: *'We'll never make that mistake again. Never. We'll never go in on the blind.'*

Indeed, their information about Minta had been correct up to a point. There was a bank of sorts here, a feed and grain on one side of it and a boarded-up store on the other, and nearby there was a freight and stage-line depot and several other old, sun-warped structures. Reeby was impressed neither by the look of the bank here nor any of these other places but he had had his instructions and he would not have fancied fronting Quint without having carried them out carefully.

Nobody in Minta took much notice of Reeby who had come in dusty and hangdog looking, in scuffed and none-too-clean clothing, seeking, so he had said to anyone he spoke to, work of any kind; but he had not been too surprised at not finding some, and indeed he had believed it to be a safe bet that there would not be any. He thought he might stop over a couple of days or so, though, to rest himself and the horse, before moving on to look elsewhere. And certainly there was nothing to distinguish him, as he had represented himself in Minta, from any one of the scores of other raggy itinerants who often came drifting through.

While he was there, however, he made it his business to get into a few casual conversations as he wandered around the grimy streets idly kicking dust; and as Quint had told him to do, he not only got a good look at the outside of the bank, but from the vantage-point of a bench right across the street, early in the day and for two days in a row, took care to note who arrived to open up and go to work. There were in fact only two of them.

At a night-camp in rough, stony country, the horses picketed, the meagre meal now over, Quint wanted to know chapter and verse. Reeby was hunkered down at the flickering fire alongside Sears who was lying on his bedroll. Quint was on his feet and so was Pearsall in his long coat, but he was wandering up and down smoking a small black cheroot.

'Well, there ain't no lawman there,' Reeby said, 'in Minta.'

'There ain't no cavalry there neither, I hope,' Sears said in a low, husky voice.

'No there ain't,' said Reeby sharply. 'In

fact there's shit-all in Minta, an' by the looks of it there'll be a lot less in its bank.'

'Tell me about the bank,' said Quint.

Reeby sat scratching under one arm. 'There's but one door. There was one at the back but it's been boarded up. There's a covered winder at the front an' there's a smaller one at the back an' it ain't got no bars nor nothin'. The whole shebang looked like it started out as somethin' else an' then got took over as a bank.'

'How many open it up an' go in?'

'Two. Ol' feller in a plug hat an' another about forty with a bad leg. Go in around eight forty-five. Not a lot happens. There was them from a freighters' an' a couple o' saloons comin' an' goin' one day, but it ain't near as big as the one at Meer's Crossin', an' God knows that warn't worth all the trouble.'

'I'll go along with that,' said Sears sourly, 'an' I reckon Hall an' Mavor would if they was here.'

'There'll be enough,' Quint said, his

51

long, brutal face strange in the dancing light of the fire.

Grunting softly, Sears eased his position, for clearly his wound was still sorely troubling him. Pearsall, the cherry star of the cheroot glowing, was pacing slowly back and forth just beyond the edge of the firelight.

'Whatever the hell we're gonna do,' Pearsall said, 'we'd best git in an' do it an' git out ag'in. I'm dead sick of all this pissin' around.'

'Well, we cain't go tonight,' said Quint, 'for it's too far. We'll pull out o' here tomorrer an' git close enough to move in on Minta after sundown.'

In the event it was well after sundown, in fact well into the late evening by the time they got near to the outskirts of the town, for progress had been slower than Quint had calculated owing to Sears having to stop and rest from time to time, none of which sat at all well with Pearsall, always a man who wanted to be on the move. Being in one place for long, according to Pearsall, was to invite problems. 'Stay a day,' Pearsall would sometimes say, 'an' they'll give yuh the once-over; stay two an' they'll start noticin' things. Stay three an' they'll start probin' an' pryin' an' askin' questions.' He stared at the back of Reeby's head as though to start on that line once again, but then didn't. These beliefs, however, had produced in Pearsall a restlessness that would not easily be stilled, whether or not strangers were around to notice him, as though being constantly on the move was the only safe and worthwhile thing to be doing.

There was only a faint light in the night sky, starlight, when they came jingling to a halt, the horses blowing and nodding, and Quint sitting with gloved hands clasped on the saddle-horn, Sears sitting with one of his hands pressed against his side. There were pale lights, too, in Minta, sufficient to offer a first impression of the place, which in Pearsall's case was, 'Jesus!'

'Move on,' said Quint then, and they did, coming to a halt again less than a hundred yards short of the nearest building, a livery, and there they dismounted and, leaving Sears with the horses, the three others went forward afoot, Reeby in front showing the way.

Around the back of the bank building which, as Reeby had promised, was a not-over-large, weather-worn structure, Quint stepped up close to feel around the frame of the single window while Reeby and Pearsall kept a look-out behind. Faintly they could hear the sound of a piano and occasionally a harmonica, perhaps both inside one of the saloons.

Presently Quint muttered to Reeby who thereupon took off his bandanna, folded it over and held it against the dark oblong of glass, near the bottom. Quint drew his long pistol and tapped the barrel sharply against the taut cloth. At the first tap nothing happened but at the second there came a sharp, splitting crack; then when Quint tapped a third time there was the sound of a piece of glass falling inside the room and breaking. They all stood still, listening; then Pearsall moved slowly to the corner of the building to take a cautious look. After a little time he said, 'Go on.'

Reeby stood away while Quint, still using the barrel of the pistol, cleared away the jagged edges of glass, then reached in and unlatched the window. To Reeby he said, 'Best go on back an' tell Sears to take 'em into the brush well out o' sight, now that we're as good as in. Here...' He took from a fob pocket in his pants a smoothly-worn silver watch and handed it to Reeby. 'He'll need this so he'll know to bring 'em up behind here afore nine, that's unless we git what we want without waitin', in which case we'll go tell him. When yuh done that, come back, an' come back careful. An' tell the bastard not to lose that watch.'

Reeby left. Pearsall came closer and gave Quint a boost up over the sill.

By the time Reeby returned and made his presence known and got into the bank with them, Quint and Pearsall had split a panel in a locked but flimsy internal door and were engaged in making an aperture big enough to reach through and unlock it. A few minutes after that they were moving around inside the main room of the place, striking matches from time to time, coming upon a sturdy safe in the process but failing to discover its keys anywhere, or keys of any sort for that matter, though they looked thoroughly through every drawer and inside every cupboard.

'Well, that's it,' Quint said at last, 'we jes' got to wait.' To Reeby he said, 'Sears understand what he's got to do?'

'Yeah.' Reeby sniffed and added, 'Reckons he's cold out there.'

'He'll git a damn sight colder a damn' sight quicker if he don't look after that watch,' said Quint. 'Well, boys, we'd best settle down an' wait for the bastards to show up with the keys.'

So they stretched out on the floor, all three, Pearsall wrapping his long coat around himself, and prepared to wait out the night.

FIVE

Naked, Jago raised the shade. Argon lay quiet in the night. This house stood right at the far end of the town, the house of a seamstress, Millie Porter, a little apart from its nearest neighbour, a few scrawny trees around it.

Jago, silhouetted against the grey outer light, moved aside, fumbled among cast-off clothing, and presently a match flared brightly as he lit a cigar and the unseen smoke spread its sweet scent through the room. Again the man's head and powerful shoulders appeared against the pale oblong of the window.

In the rumpled bed the black-haired woman lay against a mess of pillows watching him, her creamy-skinned body faintly outlined in the dimness of the room, long-limbed, heavy-breasted. She saw Jago, big, muscular, lean towards the window itself and there was a sudden creaking sound as he raised it a few inches, admitting a tongue of cool air, dissipating the enclosed stuffiness and the cigar smoke.

Several weeks had gone by since the death of Restall, and daily life in Argon had settled back into the mundanities of ordinary routine. But on the streets and in the saloons they had all seen a good deal of Matt Orford, him glad-handing, seeing and being seen, a style quite unlike that of Restall who had tended to maintain a low-key but nonetheless firm control; if Restall were to be seen striding purposefully along Main with a serious cast to his features it had been universally understood that the most prudent course was to make yourself scarce. And Restall had been of that nature and those habits even in advanced age, in fact right up until a few weeks before his final illness.

The woman had made a remark about Orford and this different way of his, but so many minutes had elapsed in silence that she had thought that Jago was not going to comment. But now he said, 'I'll let the little bastard strut awhile an' then I'll rein him in.'

'If he gets used to the strutting he might not *want* to be reined.' Millie's voice was low, slightly husky.

'Then what he wants an' what he'll get will be two real different things,' Jago assured her.

'I heard they were still putting that man Gates' name around,' Millie said then, knowing the remark would be guaranteed to provoke him, and she was not about to be disappointed.

Jago said loudly, 'That goddamn' surly sodbuster! He was allers right up Restall's ass! Well, he won't git no hearin' now. There's somethin' not right about that bastard, but I can't pin down what it is.'

'He's a friend o' Charlie Redwine's too, so I hear.'

'There's another one,' said Jago heavily. 'A slimy-mouthed drunk that's got a bad habit o' stickin' his lawyer's nose in too many things that ain't any o' his damn' business. Yeah, he's real close with Gates.

It was him that started soundin' off about Gates fer the lawman's job, an' afore Restall got a chance to go cold.'

'But why Gates? Why would Redwine pick him?'

'How in hell would I know how Redwine's mind works? But with Redwine, drunk or sober, yuh'd never be sure o' nothin'. All mouth. What he knows an' who he knows. Been all over the east, so he says; an' all over the west, no doubt lookin' an' talkin' an' shinin' up to one body or another, long afore he come to Argon.'

'They do say he's a real clever man, Ranse.'

'He's sure got a clever mouth, but one day the booze is gonna wash what wits he does have right onto one o' my tables, an' when it happens I'll put that Gates to cleanin' 'em up with Redwine's shirt.'

'You dead sure it's the reason you got such a down on Gates, that he's a friend o' Redwine's?'

'What?' Surprised, for a moment he had

failed to latch onto the significance of what she had said.

'It's just that I thought that the schoolteacher, Stella Freeman, 's been seen flickin' them big eyes o' hers at Gates.'

She could not actually see his facial expression to gauge what effect that had on him, but he turned from the window having tossed the partly-smoked cigar outside. 'What about Stella Freeman?'

'Oh, come on, Ranse, I'm not stupid. I've seen you watchin' her goin' by. She's gettin' you all out in hives, boy. Too bad she's got the hots for Gates.'

'Leave it,' Jago said.

She did. She had learned long ago just how far she could push him, even in a light tone. In fact, Millie figured that of all the people around Argon she was probably the only individual who would dare push Ranse Jago even as far as that. She had heard on good authority that limbs had been broken for much less than what she had just said to him.

Jago came pacing back to the bed and

sat down on the edge, slapping one of her rounded thighs lightly, as near as he could ever get to playful. 'Well, it sure enough ain't her bed I'm in, Mill.'

'Nor in mine,' she said.

'Then we'll soon see about that, girl,' said Jago and swung his legs up onto the bed. But what she had been saying about Gates, and in particular linking his name with Stella Freeman's, well, maybe that was the final nudge that he had needed.

It was several days after that when Gates found it necessary to drive the wagon into Argon to pick up several things he had ordered and to pay a visit to the bank. While in there he had spoken to the serious, suet-faced James Fleury and then had passed a few casual words with the dark-haired young man, Jay Lanyon; but only a few, for Fleury was well known to be quite tetchy about time-wasting and was not beyond lecturing Lanyon about such matters, if he thought it warranted, even in the presence of other people. So to avoid any embarrassment of that sort, Gates did not tarry, but he did say, 'I've talked with your ma today an' I'm invited for supper. See you then.'

It was now late in the afternoon and there was little heat left in the day, heavy cloud having slowly invaded, then captured the sky. From the wagon Gates took a studded denim jacket and shrugged it on. A slight cool breeze had begun to spring up and under the sullen sky Main had taken on a desolate look and had all but cleared of people. Little whorls of dust went spinning along as Gates crossed the street and, hands in the pockets of his jacket, went tramping up the external stairs to Redwine's office and found the attorney alone and working at his desk.

In a matter of moments Redwine had reached into a cupboard and produced a bottle and shot-glasses; so they sat there sipping the fiery drink and chewing the fat for a while. Soon, Gates asked, 'How's Matt Orford handling it?' Though he thought he could imagine how that would be.

Redwine emitted a sharp hiss of irritation. 'A peacock!' he said. 'A preening peacock.' His reddened, pouched eyes sought Gates'. 'Oh, Orford will get along just fine so long as no real trouble blows up here, or that's what I think, Dave. And I don't mean, necessarily, that if it did the boy would show no courage. But I am inclined to believe that he's the sort to show a good mix of stupidity along with it, and that could get him shot, maybe even killed and worse, it could put others at risk.'

Gates nodded slowly, turning the shot-glass between thumb and forefinger, sensing that there was something more, and asked, 'You still been putting my name around this town, Charlie?'

Caught off guard, Redwine then did his best to look contrite. 'Well, Dave, in the course of a few drinks I might have said a word or two. I apologize. I know I ought to keep my mouth shut on the subject. It's just that I believe they've made a mistake with Orford. Saving money is most likely the underlying reason. All I hope is that, one day, none of the people in this town will come to suffer for it.' For another moment, staring intently at Gates, it did seem that he was about to say more, then decided not to and poured another drink instead. Gates cupped a leathery hand over his own glass, shaking his head gently.

'I'm due over at Bess Lanyon's for supper, Charlie, so I've got to be on my best behaviour.'

'Understood,' Redwine said. 'I guess you wouldn't want to fall over in front of anybody.'

The remark was slight but the inference was not lost on Gates. 'You assume a lot, Charlie.'

'I do get drunk, but that means only that my faculties are impaired for a time, not lost irretrievably.'

'Let's leave it.'

'As you wish.' Then the bantering tone that Redwine had adopted was replaced by a more serious one. 'I've got a feeling that Jago, for one, is just biding his time with Matt Orford, allowing him to run for a while, then when it suits him he'll let him know, now that Restall's no more, where the real muscles are in Argon. Jago's a very ambitious man. He's got his eye on a lot of land around here, I'm sure of that, though I'm not divulging professional confidences, because he doesn't deal with me. So if what I think will happen does happen, we will all acquire a *de facto* lawman and maybe a few unsworn deputies as well, out there in the dark. If it came right down to it, Dave, Orford would never be able to stand up to Jago, for he simply hasn't got the moral fibre.'

'I expect that means the sand,' murmured Gates.

'Yes,' said Redwine, 'it does.' He certainly looked less than happy.

'It's time I was on my way,' Gates said. 'I thank you for the talk and for the drink, Charlie.'

Pouring another one for himself, Redwine looked across at him seriously. 'Take care of yourself Dave. Take care of yourself.'

The oddly uneasy feeling that the visit to Redwine's office had engendered was driven away to some extent by the warmth of the welcome at the Lanyons' house; yet in all the easy conversation across their supper table, Gates became conscious of a certain concern, even here, about Argon and the way that the people here had started to become uncomfortable and unsure, now that the long-familiar figure of old George Restall was no longer moving confidently among them.

'There's a saying,' Bob Lanyon remarked, his lined, squarish face serious, his pale eyes thoughtful, 'that a good man's never appreciated until he's no longer around, an' I reckon it's a true one.'

As grey as her husband, but of a less serious mien, Bess fetched more coffee to refill the cups while Stella cleared away some of the dishes. A tall woman, Stella, she was striking to look at, though not beautiful, with rich brown hair and eyes that certainly were much closer to mauve than blue. She was perhaps thirty years old, yet with a slim and firmly-rounded body, and a girl's light way of moving. Stella had lived here with her kin, the

Lanyons, for a number of years, her own parents dead long ago, apart from a spell in the east at a teaching academy. There had been stories—as even Gates had become aware—that during her absence there had also been some kind of association with a man who, in the finish, had turned out to have a wife already. So Stella Freeman, hurt and disillusioned, had returned to Argon and the bosom of the Lanyons' home, there to remain, so everyone supposed, for the rest of her life, a spinster. She had kept to her teaching, for which she had special talents, and kept her own counsel, and had deftly, though quite firmly at times, underscored the fact that a spinster she was and a spinster she had chosen to remain. Until Gates, that was; until the appearance of that quiet man had set a good few of the tongues going. But that was all that it had been—talk. And in the fullness of time, for Stella herself and for Gates, a few courteous but undeniably warm exchanges across the Lanyons' friendly table. The Lanyons knew that there was something more there though, sensed it. Young Jay Lanyon in particular, his brown eyes sometimes flicking from one to the other when they themselves seemed unaware. But now, following his father's remarks about Orford, the young man said, 'Mr Fleury, he's kind of jumpier than usual right now.'

Bob Lanyon raised his eyebrows. 'Jim Fleury?'

Bess glanced around at her son. 'Jay, it's not right to fetch tales home from the bank.'

'It's not *about* the bank, ma, not about bank business, but just how Mr Fleury seems to feel now that Sheriff Restall isn't around any more.'

'I take it,' said Gates, 'he doesn't have the same faith in Matt Orford.'

'Well, you know Mr Fleury, he doesn't come right out and say as much,' Jay said, 'but yes, that's about what it is, Dave; and something else he doesn't say, because he doesn't have to, is that one or two of Jago's men make him very uncomfortable, now that there's only Matt Orford on the streets.'

Gates was aware of the prideful looks that the elder Lanyons sometimes gave their son, a boy born when both were almost middle-aged, and who from an early age had shown that he had a sharp mind and that he might aspire to something more than a lifetime of manual work as would most of the youngsters with whom he had grown up. And the quiet pride of the parents had been justified when the banker, reputed to be a severe judge where his own business was concerned, Brophy, had taken Jay on to work under the old, sometimes very demanding James Fleury, who *was* in a sense, the Argon Bank and Loan. Until the hiring of young Lanyon he had run the place, with Brophy, using only the afternoon help of an elderly clerk and two women.

What Jay Lanyon had just said echoed strangely what Redwine had also remarked to Gates only a matter of a couple of hours ago; and though conversation now moved on to less serious topics, for Gates, all that had been said both here and in Redwine's office served only to stir to life again those feelings he had had upon leaving the town right after Restall's funeral, and which, cumulatively, amounted to a growing conviction that he ought to withdraw from any close involvements here in Argon. Whatever might come to pass in this town was not his concern, for he had not journeyed to this part of the country seeking simply to become absorbed into a community, inevitably to become entangled in its problems and in the lives of its people. On the contrary, this had been a deliberately solitary pilgrimage, Gates seeking a place where he might fashion a life for himself unencumbered by the travails of the greater world outside.

Leaving the Lanyon house a little before mid-evening, Stella had come with him to the porch, Gates conscious of the warm nearness of her and of the sweet scent she had on; but Gates' mood was continuing to oppress him, and though their goodnights seemed momentarily to promise more, there was no contact, not even the slightest touch of fingers, no matter how plainly both of them sensed the presence of feelings for which, ultimately, no words were found.

Driving the flat-decked wagon away towards the trail out of Argon, he was but sixty yards from the Lanyons' house and immersed in his own thoughts when they came at him out of the darkness.

There were two of them, reeking of whiskey, running alongside the wagon, one on either side, then catching hold to come swinging aboard. Even before they got close to him and even in the encompassing night he realized who they were: Mellish, partly bald, and Culp, hard, bony, with collar-length, dirty black hair, both of them men who appeared to be on one of Jago's payrolls, but who on the face of it did little to earn their keep, drinking a good deal, but being often in Jago's company.

Confused, the mare came to a stop. Gates took a blow to the side of the head and tried to roll away onto the deck of the wagon. But the attack had come too quickly, and because his mind had been occupied with other things he had been taken by surprise. He did fight back, trying to get to his feet up on the wagon-deck, and lashing out caught one of them a blow, sending him half off the vehicle; but the other smashed a teak-like fist into a cheekbone and bright flares went dancing in Gates' vision even as another punch caught him on the side of the jaw and he went down off the wagon to fall heavily to the ground. Only faintly did he hear one of them breathing hard somewhere above him, saying, 'Keep clear of Argon, mister. There won't be no second time of askin'.'

A bright light burst into Gates' puffed-up eyes and he tried to turn his head aside but could not, and he was unaware that a full five minutes had gone by since his body had struck the ground and that this light from which he could not escape was in fact a lamp being held by Bob Lanyon, and the hands that were holding his shoulders were those of Lanyon's son.

The elder man said, 'Let's get him up on the wagon. We'll take him back to the house that way.'

The next thing that Gates was aware of was the soft, warm-water sponging of his face by Bess Lanyon and it was her round, kindly, concerned face that now came into focus. Stella was there too, now handing Bess a dry cloth, and then his burst face was being patted softly dry, and a salve was being applied.

'I don't know if anything's broke, Dave,' Bess said. 'We should get Doc Brill over here to have a look.'

In an absurd mimicry of the long-gone Restall, he heard his own pain-husky voice saying to her, 'No, Bess... I'll be all right.'

'Who was it?' Jay asked.

Gates had to take several long, laboured breaths before he could manage to say, 'Two of Jago's men.'

'Jago's?' Bess said. 'But why?'

Stella's eyes dropped. Gates could see her more clearly now. A faint flush had come into her face. She knew why, even if Bess did not. She knew, just as Gates did. Under the solid beating of his pain Gates began telling himself that indeed this

74

was it, the culmination of all his earlier misgivings, the time to pull out—first out of Argon, then right out of this country. Perhaps Stella, looking on now that Bess had carried the bowl of pink-tinged water away, could read it in his ravaged face, for something like a shadow passed across hers and she glanced away in confusion. It was as though some delicate strand that once might have joined them had now been broken.

SIX

There could be no doubt that though the pickings, as Reeby had predicted, had been poor, Minta had in all other respects been a success. In the future, looking at Minta in retrospect however, it might be considered that it had been too easy. Not long afterwards, Pearsall had even given voice to this opinion.

'That bank,' Pearsall had said, 'was a

goddamn' matchbox. A bank that *was* a bank would be a different can o' beans altogether.'

Quint, however, had been convinced that he had now got onto an idea which had endless possibilities, so had no intention of being swerved from it. He had insisted that it was a matter of always taking a careful look at what lay in front of them before they went in anywhere. The cold spectre of the detachment of cavalry at Meer's Crossing clearly still haunted Quint and was likely to do so for some time. And after Minta he had added, 'An' next time, if there's secure bars all 'round, an' no other way in, then we leave it an' move on to look over some other place.'

By this time Reeby was back from a town named Purdue and this question of barred windows now became an important one.

They had made a camp in among some large, black rocks some twenty miles from Purdue, sheltering there from a cutting wind as much as hiding their presence. Sears, the flesh on either side of his wound now proud and reddened, was still mostly lying around and Quint, observing him in recent times, wondered how long it would be before Sears became an out-and-out liability.

Now Reeby advanced his opinion on the Purdue bank, and the town of Purdue.

'They got a lawman there but he don't look up to much.'

'Where's he live?' asked Quint at once. 'An' how far from the bank?'

'He's got a place out back o' the jail,' said Reeby, a good hundred yards from where the bank's at.' Then he said, 'Sure, the bank looks tougher'n Minta, but I reckon we can git in the same way, even though there's some bars.'

Pearsall looked up at this mention of bars and Quint said, 'Where are they, inside or outside?'

'Inside,' Reeby said, 'but at one o' the back winders I could see real plain that two of 'em is near to rusted through.' From one of his saddlebags he produced a black steel pinch-bar. 'Picked this here up in Purdue.'

Quint took hold of it and examined the curved, claw end of the bar and nodded his approval, but if he was surprised by Reeby's initiative he forbore to say so and handed the tool back to him. By this time too, while in the town, Reeby had well known what had been expected of him and now he gave the other facts that Quint was waiting to hear.

'One feller arrives at eight-twenty, an' another, the head man I reckon, around eight forty-five.'

'The question is,' Pearsall said, 'which one of 'em's got the keys we need?'

'My bet is that it's the first one there,' said Quint, 'otherwise why go in ahead o' the next feller? He's too early to set up fer the day, that's what I think.'

Reeby said, 'Two days in a row I watched 'em, same as Minta.'

'So,' said Quint, 'say ten minutes from us gettin' ahold o' the keys to bein' ready to leave. No, say fifteen. Sears brings the horses in around eight thirty-five. We'll be out an' away afore the other bastard gits there.'

'Let's hope it's gonna be worth the gittin',' Pearsall muttered.

'It looks a whole lot better'n Minta,' Reeby said.

'Anything,' said Pearsall, 'would sure look better'n Minta.'

'Picked up somethin' else in Purdue,' Reeby said, possibly seeing his opportunity to put forward an idea which seemed to him to be in all ways superior to Purdue. 'They do say that feller Restall, down there in Argon, he's dead.'

Quint looked up sharply. 'George Restall? Never met up with him but I heard a whole lot about him. Yuh sure about that?'

'Yep. An' from what a stage-line feller in Purdue was sayin', all they got now in Argon is some wet-behind-the-ears boy that's tryin' to fill Restall's boots.'

'Now that,' said Pearsall, 'is a real interestin' piece o' news. That's a sizeable place, that Argon, or so I hear.'

'So what yuh reckon?' Reeby asked, encouraged, looking at Quint, meaning why not just forget about Purdue and strike away south-west, to Argon.

'We don't know nothin' about the Argon bank,' Quint said, 'but we do know somethin' about the Purdue bank.'

'I dunno,' Pearsall said, clearly beginning to become impatient, 'I'm all fer us stoppin' pissin' around with matchboxes that's full o' peanuts. If we're gonna stick out our necks then we oughta stick 'em out fer a real hatful an' then light out fer other parts, like Mexico.'

Quint was walking slowly back and forth. Reeby, he could always manipulate. Sears was almost totally concerned with the worsening pain of his wound, so now did not count. Pearsall, however, had a mind of his own and had a history of dangerous unpredictability. If they were going to hit any bank anywhere, then Quint needed Pearsall. The loss of Hall and Mavor at Meer's Crossing had been near disastrous.

Quint, however, now turned to the immediate question of Sears and asked, 'What's it to be? Yuh gonna wait here or what?'

'No,' Sears said, easing his body over, seeking some new position which might afford him less discomfort. 'If it all turned to shit I'd never know about it, stuck out here. No, I'll come on to Purdue an' watch out fer the horses. If it's gonna be Argon, I dunno. It's a helluva ways, Argon.'

Quint sniffed and rubbed at his stubbly jaw, then nodded. Reeby and Pearsall looked critically at Sears but said nothing. Sears, however, thought that if Quint was so minded, if he should come to believe that Sears might at some crucial point become a liability, he would put him down like a rabid dog.

SEVEN

Redwine was not yet so drunk that he did not come to realize that they had been watching him, taking particular notice of him, and by this time the whispers that on a recent night the sodbuster, Gates, had run afoul of some hard men had spread around Argon. Redwine had not been slow to lay the blame for that right at his own door, and the hurt was an almost palpable thing.

Now, sitting in his office, a whiskey bottle at hand, he was trying to put between himself and that unpalatable belief of guilt a gentling cushion of alcohol, though Redwine was equally aware that the perceived link between Gates and Stella Freeman might well have had some influence on what had happened to Gates. The fight, which it appeared no-one else had witnessed, was being put around Argon, however, as just another drunken brawl, though Redwine did not believe a word of that for he felt that he knew Dave Gates much too well; and anyway, on that night, in this very office, Gates himself had quietly refused a second drink; and Gates, as Redwine also knew, would have been highly unlikely to have been offered anything stronger than coffee over at Bob Lanyon's house. So this tale of a drunken brawl was clearly one that someone had been actively promoting, and Redwine, while conceding probable prejudice, was convinced that it would have come from Ranse Jago. No, Redwine felt he *knew* it to be so. Others, however, beyond people like the Lanyons, would not. He closed his eyes and with his long fingers pressed blue-veined temples, his head beginning to buzz faintly from the effects of the whiskey.

First he heard their boots hammering on the outside stairs and he did not even have time to get out of his chair—for all the good it would have done—before the door was banging back on its hinges, shuddering, and they were inside the room, both men with their greasy hats hanging on leather thongs against their backs: Mellish, freckled, balding with remnants of reddish hair, and Culp, the rangy, bony man, his wild, dark hair bunching thickly over his collar. They stank of stale sweat.

Redwine did manage to get to his feet and Culp then reached both hands across the desk, seizing the attorney by the jacket and hauling him bodily over, while Mellish rescued the wobbling whiskey bottle. The shot-glass, however, sent tumbling to the floor, survived and went rolling away.

'Now,' Culp said, 'this is where yuh git a lesson in manners an' mindin' your own goddamn' business, Mr Charlie Redwine.'

Culp took the bottle away from his mouth. 'Like your good friend Gates got.'

Still holding Redwine's jacket bunched in his fists, Mellish suddenly snapped his head forward against Redwine's nose which at once spurted blood, then Mellish lifted him bodily and sat him on the desk, slamming him down hard, the attorney's arms flailing limply.

'First,' Culp said, wiping his mouth with the back of a hand, 'we got to have a little talk.'

Redwine's head was ringing, his nose streaming blood, the effects of the whiskey he had drunk all but overcome by the pain he was now feeling; and in Mellish's strong hands he was completely helpless. When Mellish suddenly released him, Culp at once took hold of him, Mellish now taking the whiskey and gulping some of it, then allowing breath to hiss out from between his teeth as the fiery spirit went coursing through him.

'This here Gates bastard,' Culp said, 'this great friend o' yourn, there was questions he shoulda been asked, an' wasn't, an' the first of 'em is, where'd he come from, this greasy sodbuster?'

Gasping for breath, Redwine managed to say, 'I...don't know...'

While Culp held him, Mellish, still gripping the bottle in one hand, stepped closer and hit Redwine hard in the side of the face with the other.

'Yuh deef, attorney? Where'd he come from?' When Culp decided that Redwine would not answer, though in fact he could not, for he was now slipping away from full consciousness, Culp nodded, releasing Redwine, and Mellish now hit him hard in the midriff, sending the attorney crashing back across the desk to entangle himself in the chair, so that it and he went slamming against the wall, bringing Redwine's framed diploma down, the glass shattering when it struck the floor.

When Redwine's awareness began more or less to come back it was to the realization that he was vomiting on the floor, the sour stench overpowering the whiskey-smell and the smell of these appalling men.

Mellish came pacing unhurriedly around the desk and took hold of Redwine's collar and dragged him round to the centre of the room. Culp, standing over Redwine, then kicked him very hard in the side, Redwine crying out and rolling away in agony, finishing face down. Culp calmly worked one of his boots in under the prone man and, giving a grunting heave, flopped him over onto his back, fetching another hoarse cry from Redwine.

'Now we got to start all over,' Mellish said, swigging again from the bottle.

'An' if we don't like what we hear,' said Culp, 'we'll boot your ribs clean out your ass, mister, an' then when we done that, we'll ask ag'in.'

A feeble gesture of one hand that Redwine somehow managed to make was apparently sufficient to show them that he was ready to say something, for they now simply stood over him, waiting. Redwine's head and body was now a single, throbbing whole and he was, he thought, covered in blood and he sincerely believed that he would be unable to take any more pain. And the biggest fear of all was that if he continued resisting them, then there was a terrifying certainty that he would be crippled by these men, or worse. But when he tried to speak, though his swollen lips parted, no distinguishable word came out, and Mellish leaned down slightly.

'What? What was it? Where?'

Breathing harshly through his mouth, as though he had lately run a mile, Redwine made another attempt to speak, and this time was just audible. '...Wy... Wyoming...'

'Where, in Wyomin'?'

'Not...sure...' When he sensed rather than saw Culp make a move to hurt him again, he said, 'Lara...mie...'

'So, the bastard come from there, did he?'

'He was there...one time... Before that...I truly...don't know.'

'So yuh was there, in Laramie, when Gates was?'

'No...after. I was there...after. I didn't know... Gates there. Not 'til he came...to Argon.'

'So yuh tell us, mister. So yuh tell us.'

'It's true...' Redwine then seemed to drift off, as though he might be losing his tenuous grip on his senses, or perhaps believed that these men, having got this information, might now leave him; but Culp gave him a sharp nudge with a boot.

'There's somethin' that's not right about that Gates bastard,' he said, 'so yuh best start tellin' us some more, mister. What was it yuh heard about him in Laramie?'

'He'd been there...when a man...got shot and died. Gates...blamed himself... Others...blamed him as well....'

'Gates? Why Gates? Why would some damn' cloth-eared sodbuster be mixed up with some shootin'?' Mellish, green eyes very foxy, evidently thought Redwine perfectly capable of trying to deceive them in spite of their threats to him and what they had already done to him.

'He wasn't...a farmer then...'

'No? What, then?'

'He was...a marshal.'

'What?' Clearly it had been unexpected and Culp's tone said it all.

'Gates...was a marshal there.'

'But not when yuh got to Laramie?'

'No...It was all over with...by then.'

'Who was it got shot?' Culp asked. 'Anybody important?'

'I don't know the name...or can't... remember. A deputy...a young man. He got caught by armed men...in a place that Gates...had thought—no, had *said* was safe to go...into... That it...had been cleared.'

'An' then it turned out it wasn't,' Mellish muttered.

'No...it wasn't.'

'So what happened then?' Culp asked. 'They run the stupid bastard out on a rail?'

'No...well, he left... Went to Colorado, so I heard...dropped out of sight. In

Laramie there was a lot of...ill-feeling.'

'Well now,' Mellish said, scratching at his belly, 'an' now here the prick is down in Argon, turnin' dirt an' kissin' the law's ass an' all.'

Culp laughed and said, 'I bet Gates didn't figure anybody here would know about all that, an' I bet he didn't cotton to it when he found some attorney did.'

'He doesn't...even know...I've heard of it,' Redwine said in a deep whisper.

'Well now,' Mellish said again, 'won't he be in fer a goddamn' shock?'

Redwine closed his eyes. Physically hurt, he now felt mentally ravaged as well, deeply ashamed of his capitulation, his treachery, his cowardice. It seemed to him that if he had been given one chance in his lifetime to measure himself, for himself, as a man, then he had failed abysmally. Perhaps, after all, they would shoot him now. Strangely he did not fear that, only the thought of further pain.

But they did not shoot him, nor did they beat him any more; they did worse than that, they laughed at him and then they left him, sodden with his own blood, reeking of his own vomit.

In Argon, whispers were passed from lip to lip. Jago, at a window above his saloon, drawing on a cigar, stared out over Argon roofs and thought about Gates coming to grips with new knowledge of him, surprised, yet satisfied, confident that when it became widely known, Gates would do what clearly he had already done once, perhaps, for all they knew, numerous times; he would turn tail and run. After all, he had virtually been turned out of Laramie, no matter how Redwine had slimy-worded it.

Jay Lanyon overheard it while working at the bank and took it home at evening where it stilled all other talk at the supper-table. Bess pondered aloud, 'What will poor Dave do when he finds out it's common knowledge in Argon?'

Stella, her face first pale with shock, then colouring faintly, looking down at her unfinished meal, said, even as Ranse Jago had been thinking, 'Perhaps he'll not want to stay anywhere near Argon. He might just move on.'

Bess glanced quickly at her when she said that but a look from Bob Lanyon checked any comment his wife might have been about to make.

In the brief silence that followed, Jay said, 'I caught sight of Mr Redwine yesterday, and he looked as though he'd been run over by a wagon.'

'Hurt, you mean?' asked Bess. She stopped short of saying, *'Or drunk?'*

Jay nodded. 'Hurt real bad. His face was a mess and he couldn't stand up straight; and he was walking very slowly.'

Bob Lanyon steadfastly got on with his meal. If he now realized the probable truth he was not prepared to say. Stella was looking at him, he knew, but he would not look at her. He knew that she had arrived at the same conclusion. Something had made the connection for her between what had happened to Redwine and what had happened to Gates only a short distance from this very house. Perhaps, the circumstances now forgotten, she too had picked up something in the past from Charlie Redwine, a word, a hint, a suspicion, but had thought little of it.

Redwine, at the foot of his steps and about to climb stiffly up to his office, turned in the half light, having visibly started at even her light step.

'May I talk with you?'

'Of course, Miss Freeman. Do please come up.'

'No. No, I've only a few minutes, Mr Redwine. But I need to know...'

He looked down at his own shoes and there was a brief pause before he said, 'About Dave Gates? I thought perhaps you might.'

'The things that are being said—are they true?'

'That Dave Gates was once a marshal in Wyoming? Yes, quite true. I believe what I was told, up there, a few years ago.'

'And now this tale has come here, followed him here.'

His devastated expression was enough and he knew that she could read even his ill-used face. 'Yes, and it came from me, Miss Freeman. I admit to it. I can assure you I am by no means proud of it; but I have discovered—if I did not already know—that my threshold of pain is not nearly as high as I might have hoped.'

'Who was it did that to you? Will you tell me?'

'Don't allow that kind of certain knowledge to put yourself at risk, Miss Freeman.'

She would not be put off easily though. 'They were the same men who attacked Dave, weren't they?'

Still he would not answer but she knew from his very reticence that it had been so. She said, 'When you were putting Dave's name around in Argon, for peacekeeper, that was the reason? You knew he'd been a marshal once, and in a much bigger, rougher place?'

'Yes. Yes, that's true. But I'm also quite sure that Dave doesn't know I was ever there, that I recognized his name from all that time ago and a long way from this place.'

'But perhaps he does suspect it?'

He nodded, at least having to concede

that. 'He's far from being a fool, as you no doubt know. He could have guessed that I knew something. Perhaps I let something slip inadvertently. Again, perhaps not. But I have to say that the men who did this to me, seeking information about him, had no prior notion of it at all. Dave himself was attacked for quite different reasons, Miss Freeman.'

She looked at him, then away. Redwine was no fool either, so much was clear.

Gates, moving slowly between house and barn, turned when he heard the wagon, then saw it come into view some hundred yards away, on the trail out of Argon, and when he recognized the freight-line rig he relaxed. Griffiths, heading up to Purdue.

Upon seeing Gates' wave, the wagoner drew his four-horse team to a halt, waiting for the homesteader to come painfully towards him, and by the time Gates arrived, Griffiths having rolled a skinny smoke, was puffing contentedly.

It was from this amiable man, then, that he learned that Charles Redwine had somehow fallen foul of men he could not or would not identify; and now there was all this talk around Argon about Gates himself, about some shooting or other, years back, when Gates was supposed to have been a marshal up in Wyoming.

There was no malice in Griffiths though, nor did he seem to realize, either, the effect that it might have on Gates. 'Yuh sure are a deep one, Dave.'

After the wagon had gone grinding away Gates had the distinct impression that Griffiths had thought it all some kind of hoax.

EIGHT

Redwine had not expected to see him, but even though it was after sundown thought it prudent to get in off the street.

'If you can manage to get up these steps,' he said, 'I can. Just. My God, Dave, we're a sight to see, the pair of us.'

Gates followed him slowly up the stairs and eventually into the office.

'Best leave the lamps off. You can never tell what kind of moths they'll attract.'

'Understood.' Redwine nodded. 'I'll raise the shades though, but mind where you step. You know, Dave, if these walls could speak, they'd have a story to tell.' Obviously Redwine was having trouble talking and was probably putting a brave face on this meeting. Gates went right to the heart of the matter.

'It was Culp, wasn't it? And Mellish?'

There was no equivocation. 'Yes. But when they came here to me, it was for a different reason.'

Gates did not attempt to evade the matter. 'It's true that in my case it was more than likely on account of Stella Freeman. I know it, maybe others do too, that Jago's eye likes to rove in that quarter.' He shook his head when Redwine, raising his eyebrows, pointed to a bottle. 'But yeah, I hear they came to talk to you about other things.'

'Dave, I simply can't begin to tell you

how bad I feel about it.' Nor could he. The reality of what he had done, exposing another individual to opprobrium and quite possibly to more physical harm, had been gnawing at Redwine ever since.

'Charlie, if you hadn't told those two bastards what they'd been sent here to find out, the very least they'd have done, in the finish, would have been to bust your legs. You might never have climbed your steps out there again, Charlie.'

'Believe me, I did come to that probability quite quickly; but it doesn't make me feel one whit better.' Redwine could not conceal from Gates that he was deeply disturbed and ashamed.

Gates had to ask, however, 'When were you in Laramie?'

'I guess it was about a month after you'd moved on. As it happened I wasn't there for long.' That was certainly true. A bout of drinking had affected some work he was engaged in there and he had had to leave in a kind of shame.

'But long enough. I can understand that people there would have still been stirred up; but it seems to me you weren't about to mention it here in Argon, Charlie, not even to me.'

'I received information without having sought it and I considered it to be none of my business.' What a paltry thing to salvage from dishonour, Redwine thought.

Gates nodded but he said no more on the subject except to ask, 'When you were in Laramie, did you ever meet any people called Jensen?'

Redwine, staring at him in the gloom, thankful that his face was shadowed, nodded. 'Yes.' Then, 'What will you do now?'

'If I stayed anywhere near Argon and had to come into town, they'd make sure this wasn't just allowed to die. If things got worse—an' I reckon they would—I'd likely end up blasting one of 'em an' then maybe somebody that didn't deserve it would get themselves hurt, like you got hurt. No way is it worth it, an' God only knows what might happen then. No, I'm here tonight to see Evan Leeder, to try to sell up my outfit; that, an' to talk with the

Lanyons an' with Stella, an' tell them all the truth of it, straight. It's the very least I owe them after all the kindnesses they've shown me.'

'Leeder's not in Argon right now,' Redwine had to tell him. 'I hear he's gone up to a place outside Spanjer on land sale business.' Gates was disappointed and it showed, and Redwine said, 'He's due back in Argon in a couple of days. Dave, if you want, I can get him to come out and see you.'

'I'd sure be obliged, Charlie,' Gates said. He turned to leave then, but pulled up as though cramped.

'Are you all right?' Redwine asked.

'In at least as good shape as Charlie Redwine. I'm going over to Bob Lanyon's now.' He had badly wanted to ask Redwine the same question, for there had been something in the man's face that had worried Gates. He held back, but he did say, 'Take care of yourself, Charlie.'

Redwine said, 'I ought to have done better than that before now. I've owned this thing for years but never ever tried to use it.' He lifted something from a drawer and Gates could just see the dull gleam of what looked like an old army pistol.

Gates said, 'Whether it's loaded or not, if you'd tried for it, Charlie, they'd have killed you.'

Gates got away from Main as soon as he could, passing to a darker back street by which he could walk through to the Lanyon house. He had not gone far before, up ahead, perhaps eighty feet from him, he could hear and then just see a lone figure approaching, and something about the way of walking made Gates go tense and strain to pierce the gloom. Recent happenings had made him wary. And just as well. While indeed, in Argon, Gates would always move cautiously now, after what had happened to him there, others, for those same reasons, would likely not expect to see him there.

Culp certainly didn't, for Gates recognized the man at a distance of a few feet, and though Gates, as he had shown in Redwine's office, was still stiff and sore from the beating he had taken, he used the vital moment of surprise to advantage, driving a fierce punch in Culp's face, a blow that carried with it nearly all of Gates' bodyweight. The smack of the punch was loud in this quiet street, and as big as he was, Culp, crying out, went down like a shot dog. Gates felt no compassion for this man, not so much for the pain that he himself had suffered at Culp's hands but for what Culp, along with Mellish, had quite systematically and without pity done to Charles Redwine.

Without hesitating, Gates now moved over the top of the dazed and moaning Culp and drove a boot into him, this time fetching a scream from the dark-headed man as he rolled over, then tried, like some gross, slow-moving grub, to crawl away from further punishment. But Gates now placed a boot on the back of Culp's head forcing the man down, the side of his face, as he twisted his head, being pressed to the ground.

'Go near any friend of mine again in Argon,' Gates said, 'an' I'll break you so you can't go near anybody again; an' tell your friend that too, from me.' He walked on, his left hand throbbing from the effects of hitting Culp as hard as he had.

Jago pulled on his shirt, moving from the bedroom towards the sound of crockery in the kitchen where Millie Porter, her black hair tumbling loosely down her back and wearing a blue robe, was making coffee. When he joined her she was still unwilling to let go what she had been probing him about earlier, risking his wrath.

'It was that Culp, wasn't it, an' Ord Mellish that beat Charlie Redwine?'

'You best go ask 'em,' Jago said, 'but stand well back when yuh do it, that's my advice.' There was less confidence in his voice though than was usual, for though he would never admit it to the woman, Jago had felt a stir of unease. Culp and Mellish could have handled it better. Things might easily have gone too far. Gates was one thing, Redwine entirely another, no matter what the gains might have been; for, drink or no drink, Redwine was regarded here in Argon, when all the chips were counted and no matter how

103

many of the prissy wives' mouths tightened over the drinking, as an able legal man, and where land and other property agreements abounded and bitter disputes over them were almost endemic, not only in Argon but in the wider country around it, a man of Charles Redwine's undisputed capabilities was worth plenty. Out here, charlatans were two bits for a set of six and in the past there had been numerous sorry experiences to point to; so Redwine, to people such as say Brophy, people who wielded influence, was a professional asset not to be cast away lightly. Even young Orford, full of himself elsewhere in Argon but circumspect when around Jago, had clearly become uncomfortable over what had happened to Redwine, as though he was aware that some people were waiting and watching to see if he would seek out who was responsible. For though Redwine himself had resolutely refused to name the men who had used him so cruelly, there were widespread and soundly-based suspicions as to who they were likely to be, and they were men who had the closest possible ties to Ranse Jago. If matters were not taken in hand, Orford might find close supporters among the town's merchants, the men who had conferred office upon him. And for once, Jago did not react too harshly now when Millie Porter said, looking at him out of her large, dark eyes, 'You should get rid of them, Ranse, not get the smell of 'em on your hands.'

'Don't you concern yourself about what I do,' he said, and in his own reactionary defence, thought, *'The hell with 'em an' their prissy-mouthed wives.'* And instead of retreating, he now firmed in his resolve to let this Orford boy know exactly where he stood before he got ideas that were too big for his hat. Gates had been dealt with. Redwine, well, maybe that had been a mistake, the way it had been done, but it had turned up good information. He must now rein Orford in.

As though she had actually read what was in his mind, she said, 'Sometimes, Ranse, you are your own worst enemy, never satisfied.'

Gates and Stella Freeman were standing

in the shadow cast by the back porch, having just come out of the Lanyon house, leaving serious, even sad faces inside. Gates had not gone into detail about Laramie, he had merely admitted that there had been an incident in that place; but Stella, now away from the others, was not so easily satisfied.

'Why do you blame yourself, Dave? For that's what it is, isn't it?'

'You had to be there,' Gates said. 'What went on there was down to me, an' whether or not, on the day, too many things were happening too fast, when the critical time came I made a mistake that should never have been made.'

She was silent for a moment or two, but then said, 'The one who was killed that day, was he related to you?'

He stiffened slightly at the directness of it, but said, 'No.' The silence ran on, so that it seemed he might not continue. 'A boy named Luke Jensen.'

'A deputy?'

'Yeah, one of my sworn deputies.'

'Dave, I'd like to know what happened.'

She stopped short of, *'At least tell me that before you go.'*

After another awkward pause, he said, 'There was a raid on a railroad freight office. There were boxes of currency in transit, held over for just a few hours. Somebody gave information. Four of 'em came in, well-mounted, well-armed, fit to spit in my eye they were, hard, bitter men, all of 'em.' For a short time he fell silent, thinking about it, finding it difficult, living through it again. 'There was a fight, one of 'em brought down, one of my men down too, leg-shot. We stopped 'em getting back to their horses an' there was a fight that went down alleys an' side-streets. It was a hell of a mess. A townsman got too close an' was shot. I still had a couple of men with me. We went ahead, building to building, clearing each one we came to. We thought we could manage to box in the men we were closing on. I sent Jensen to try to get around the side, through a place I'd already checked out.' He paused again, but briefly. 'But it turned out one of 'em was still there, a man with a rifle, an' he blew the top of Jensen's head off.'

It shocked her, but she said, 'Surely that man must have got in again somehow, after you'd been through.'

'It's a convenient answer,' Gates said. She knew that this was a reason—an excuse, he would no doubt have said—that he must have turned over in his mind a thousand times. He said, 'Afterwards I had to go tell the boy's people, his ma and pa and his sister, Annie Jensen. Me an' Annie Jensen were but two months away from our wedding.'

She did not know what to say. 'Dave—'

In the dappled dark a hand moved briefly, a gesture dismissing further talk, and he turned away, but he did say, 'I'm sorry, I should've told you long before this.'

And after he had gone, heading off to the wagon that he had left somewhere in the town, she did not immediately go back in the house but leaned her head against the side of the porch, trying to get control of all the feelings now welling up inside her. Over the weeks and months they had been drawing closer together, she and Dave Gates, and now quite quickly, whatever there had been and might have been, seemed to have vanished; not because of what he had felt disposed to tell her about the events in Laramie, not because the woman, Annie, might still be there, for Gates. He had not needed to elaborate on the truth of that, that it was behind him and had more than likely ended in fierce acrimony. It was much more likely that it had been the building of tensions here in Argon, the violence, particularly the attack on Charles Redwine, and now Gates was simply not prepared to put her or anyone else at risk because of his presence here.

On his wagon, slowly moving out of Argon, Gates had one last glimpse of life on the main street, the figure of Matt Orford striding out along the boardwalk, wearing, by the looks of it, a new, high-crowned hat, strutting, Gates thought. Well, good luck to him. Eventually he might need it.

In a seedy rooming-house not far from where Orford was walking and below whose windows Gates, on his wagon, had not long since passed, Reeby, still fully-clothed, lay on a narrow bed smoking a skinny cigarette and feeling pleased with himself. In Argon for the past three days, ostensibly resting up, taking a drink here and there, he was satisfied that he had made a careful study of the Argon Bank and Loan and its environs, and satisfied with certain tasks that he had been able to carry out. A secure place by the looks of it, a brick building, no less, with few windows, and what windows there were securely barred on the inside. No Purdue rust here. Yet Reeby was still content with his three days' work. Of the places they had hit over recent months, including Purdue, Argon looked to be the prize that Quint had been working up to. And once they had done with Argon, even Quint would have to agree that they could afford to be on easy street for some time. They could go to ground and then they could head down maybe across the border for a while.

NINE

Quint had not dismounted, nor had Reeby, nor Sears who was sitting the saddle in a hunch-shouldered, somewhat slumped attitude. Pearsall, however, had got down and was moving round in his long coat, flexing his legs.

The roofs of Argon were cut in sharp angles against the grey-dark sky, a night of combed-out cloud and little moon, night conditions as Quint had earlier observed which for their purposes could not have been better. And though only Reeby had visited this place before, and though they now knew that this one would be no simple task, Quint's questioning of Reeby had been such that they knew, too, exactly what they would be up against and what they would have to do to get inside the Argon bank; and once that had been achieved, all Sears would have to do, as he had managed to do in Purdue and Minta, was bring the horses in from their place of concealment at a prearranged time, for it was still considered to be most prudent to keep them well out of sight until they were needed. Quint, using his best judgement therefore, based on all that Reeby had told him, had declared the right time to be eight forty-five. 'An take good care o' that watch,' Quint had warned Sears.

Reeby's tale of Argon and in particular the building they would have to deal with had at first seemed to constitute a nut that would take some cracking and perhaps would even be better bypassed; but by the time he had finished, despite Pearsall's brooding scepticism and Sears' depressing, almost fatalistic acceptance of his pain-racked lot, Quint had come to see the manifold possibilities that were there, in Argon.

'Two in, usually together, at around eight-thirty, a man about fifty, name o' Fleury I found out, an' a feller a lot younger. Then the man hisself, the banker, name o' Brophy, around nine. That's all in the mornin'. The others, there's an old feller comes in about an hour after noon an' a couple o' women as well. Then they're all in there 'til the outfit shuts, around four. Busy ol' town, busy ol'bank.'

'This peacekeeper?' Quint had asked. 'What about him?' For that had been one of the whispers that had attracted them to Argon in the first place.

'Young. Twenty, about. Called Orford. Real full o' hisself, he is. No deputy nor nothin'. Spends a lot o' time walkin' up an' down Main in a fancy hat. There's more handier-lookin' fellers in this place than their damn' wet-eared sheriff.'

'Such as?'

'Man named Jago, he's got a whole lot to say. Hard man, runs a saloon an' a lumber yard. Couple o' Jago's boys could be a handful if the wind started blowin' the wrong way.'

'We'll be well away afore anybody gits a chance to be a handful,' Quint said.

'It sounds goddamn' complicated to me,' said Pearsall, having listened attentively to

Reeby throughout. He had gone off to one side to relieve himself but now came back, buttoning his pants.

'I got it worked out. I got it set up,' Reeby said.

Pearsall made a small hissing noise between his teeth to indicate what he thought about the quality of Reeby's preparations, judging by what he had heard of them so far.

Quint then directed their attention to what appeared to be a denser growth of brush over to the left of where they now were. 'We'll put 'em over there. They'll be well out o' sight.'

Reeby then explained to Sears precisely the line he would have to take to get to the back of the brick bank when the time came, explaining that he would in any case be able to see it between widely spaced structures along the back street. 'An' we'll see yuh comin',' he said.

'Right now, this is gonna leave us a helluva way to walk in,' Pearsall complained.

'Time,' said Quint, 'we got plenty of.'

Which was not really what Pearsall had meant.

Now they were standing, the open brush country behind them, for there were indeed only a scatter of buildings forming this back street on this side of Argon, only a matter of forty feet behind the bank building, but with faint lamplight spreading onto one side of it from what Reeby told them was a rooming-house, separated from the bank by an alleyway. Yet even as they stood there, someone must have pulled shades and this lamp-glow vanished. When the solid reality of the brick building stood thus before them, Pearsall could not refrain from expressing his feelings.

'Jesus!'

On the opposite side of the bank was a gap of about five feet, not as wide as the alley on the other side and impassable anyway for it was clogged with what seemed to be junk and a few pieces of lumber. The neighbouring structure on that side was built entirely of wood and like the bank also had an upper floor.

'That's the other place, there,' Reeby

said. 'That dump's empty, an' that's the one we use.'

So, led by Reeby they went pacing forward and saw that at the back of this empty building stood a small porch.

'We got to bust in here?' Pearsall enquired sourly.

'No need,' Reeby said, plainly enjoying his moment. He had his pinch-bar along but it was still slid down inside his belt. Reeby stepped up and pushed the door, which, although it gave a rasping creak, opened immediately. 'Been in this way afore,' Reeby said, 'with the pinch-bar.' He led them on in. 'Push that door shut behind you.' For the time being, through his prior knowledge, he was effectively in charge and left both Quint and Pearsall—who was carrying his shotgun—to come fumbling along behind him. Becoming accustomed to the interior gloom they proceeded, all three, in a slow, shuffling line through a room empty but for a pot-bellied stove, into a passageway, until Reeby said, 'Here's the stairs.'

Once they gained the upper floor he led

the way into another room which was bare but for two items placed there beforehand by Reeby himself, a large, empty crate which he said he had fetched from among the junk outside, and a length of lumber a foot and a half wide, about eight feet long and almost two inches thick. 'Near to bust my ass gittin' 'em up here,' Reeby said.

Until now Quint had been content to let Reeby go, but now he said, 'I hope to Christ yuh didn't let nobody see what was goin' on.'

'Naw, it was all done, like, after sundown.' A faint greyish light was filtering down on them. 'An' there's the skylight,' Reeby said.

Quint, assisted by Reeby, got himself up onto the tipped-over crate and was able to reach this skylight with ease and though, because of age and weathering, at first it seemed immovable, eventually, after a fierce, grunting effort from Quint, it rasped upwards, some old paint and not a little grit coming down on Quint on a tongue of night air.

'Thank Christ fer that,' Quint said,

spitting grit and now panting from his efforts. Eventually Quint heaved himself up through the open skylight and onto the flat roof itself.

Then began the unsteady, awkward business of manoeuvring the heavy length of lumber up through the skylight and so also onto the roof. When this had been accomplished, with Quint, above, continually appealing for care and for quiet, they took a short rest before Pearsall got up on the crate, then Reeby handed him his shotgun which in turn Pearsall passed up to Quint. Presently all three were out on the roof kneeling down and contemplating the next move and listening for any evidence that they might have been seen or heard.

From where they were, beyond a low parapet which fronted Main, they were aware of a faint glow apparently produced by the few lamps still burning in places somewhere along that street, and they could see with reasonable clarity the nearside of the bank building which was their objective.

'Ready?' Quint asked at length.

Reeby said, 'Yep,' and Pearsall merely grunted. Pearsall did not really have any sort of head for heights though it was not something he was disposed to discuss.

Slowly, all taking hold of the length of lumber, they slid it out beyond the edge of the roof across the black void of the five-foot gap until it bumped against the side of the bank. At this stage they were faced with the difficult job of lifting it slightly, for the roof of the bank, a low coping around it, was some three or four inches higher. When it was finally in position Pearsall said, 'It don't look wide enough.'

Reeby glanced at him but said nothing. Quint stood up and with one boot carefully tested the plank; then in two strides he was across on the other side. Reeby went next, then they waited for Pearsall to come. In a low voice, Pearsall said, 'Take this thing.' Reeby reached out and grasped the shotgun that Pearsall was extending.

Then when Pearsall did not move at once, Reeby said, 'Come on.'

They could see the tall figure of Pearsall in his long coat against the lighter dark of the sky and for several more seconds it seemed that he might not move; but finally he put one boot on the plank and came across with almost a leaping second stride, caught a toe on the coping and fell onto the roof of the bank and swore viciously. Then he sat up and began rubbing at one of his knees.

Quint said softly, 'Wait.' Slowly Quint went forward in a half crouch towards the low brick parapet at the front of the building and once there, he risked a look out over Main. It seemed utterly deserted and only a very few windows were showing lights, two of these at street-level, some others among upper floors. Across to his left, slivers of light showed around some of the shades in the rooming-house across the alley. Quint was on the point of turning away when he noticed someone going along the boardwalk on the opposite side of the street, a gangly figure, passing now across one of the dimly-lighted windows, the quick impression of a man in a tall, light-coloured hat and walking as though he owned the town. Perhaps, going on what Reeby had told them, that would be the new law in Argon, whose name Reeby had also told them but which Quint could not for the moment remember.

Still crouching, Quint came shuffling back to them to find both Reeby and Pearsall examining the skylight which Reeby had earlier said was on the roof of the bank building and had been revealed to him when he had stood on his bed in the rooming-house.

'So here we are,' Reeby said. He was bending over now trying to work the flat end of his pinch-bar in between the glass-frame and its solid, raised surround but not immediately managing to do it.

'Yuh might have to bust the glass,' said Pearsall.

'Which might jes' be heard as far away as Purdue,' Quint said. Then, 'What was the name o' that boy that's got the badge?'

'Orford,' said Reeby, still manipulating the pinch-bar. 'Why?'

'I think it was him I jes' seen paradin' along Main, so keep it real quiet.' Even as he said this there was a sharp snapping noise and Reeby swayed forward and nearly fell through the glass and perhaps would have if Pearsall had not grabbed an elbow and held it firmly.

'Shit!' said Reeby.

Lifting the skylight open was not easy for the hinges were stiff, clogged with dirt, so that when they did get it raised the framed glass stood upright and Quint said to leave it in that position. It was not possible to see what might lie below that a man would drop onto after lowering himself down inside. Nevertheless Reeby, handing his pinch-bar to Pearsall, turned his body and, grasping the edge of the skylight frame, did lower himself into the darkness and when his arms were fully extended, hung there for a moment before letting go and dropping the rest of the way. The rest of the way turned out to be some three feet and he landed on bare boards, slipped, and made thumping sounds as he went sprawling, hitting one hand against something solid. 'Shit!' said Reeby.

Looking up, he could see the hatted heads of Quint and Pearsall limned against the sky. Reeby then raked around in one of his pockets. 'Stay still,' he said, 'I'm gonna light a match.' Before Quint could pass judgement on that there was a scratching noise and the sudden flare of a match-flame, bringing into view a couple of broken chairs and several wooden cabinets with deep drawers in them—it had been one of these that Reeby had knocked his hand against. The match flame died.

Quint, after some rustling and grunting, was then suspended and dropped, keeping his feet on landing. Pearsall's voice said, 'Can yuh see this? Pinch-bar.' He let it go and Quint clutched it to him. Then Pearsall said, 'Here.' This was the shotgun. Quint took the barrel end of it, and then Pearsall, his long coat rustling, lowered himself down and dropped into the room.

Quint crossed to the door and went out

onto the landing to stand there listening, then came back in. They could now distinguish each other more easily in the gloom and could just see where the chairs and cabinets were. Quint said, 'We'll move one o' them things in under the skylight, because now we got to shut it.'

The nearest one of the tall cabinets was heavier than they had bargained for but between them they wrestled it to the middle of the room and then boosted Reeby with his pinch-bar to the top of it.

By reaching up he just managed to hook the curved end of the bar over the open skylight's edge and draw it down with surprisingly little noise from the clogged hinges, and because they were clogged it did not fall abruptly. Nevertheless Quint fretted some about what noise there was.

Down on the ground floor they felt their way around, not risking a match down here. After a little while, coming along behind high counters with brass grilles and trimmings, eventually, after blundering against office furniture, they arrived at what they had been seeking, though it turned out to be not a large safe, but what clearly was a small, steel-doored vault.

'Well,' Quint said, 'so here she is, boys. This here's the tin can they're gonna fetch us the key to, by an' by.'

Pearsall laid his shotgun on the floor and eased himself down as well.

Reeby said, 'We got a long time to wait.' He pointed.

On the wall above the vault was a large round clock with its Roman numerals just discernible in the gloom.

'It'll pass soon enough,' said Quint.

'Five spots says the boy's the first one through the door,' said Reeby.

'An' my five says he ain't,' said Pearsall.

'Might as well stretch out where we're at,' said Quint. He was thinking now about Sears who had made real hard work of getting this far, and if, this one last time in this strip of country, he could be relied upon to get the horses in back of the place at just the right time; or at all.

TEN

Late in the evening or not, Sheriff Orford, in the splendid awareness of his sworn office as keeper of the peace, was approaching the saloon, the Spanish Girl, owned by Ranse Jago, obeying a compulsion that had been building in him as week had followed week, to make clear this authority he had in Argon and to send a message to those who, in recent times in particular, had been known to be making light of it.

At this hour, for want of enough customers, the saloon was shut and the town itself lay quietly in this near-moonless night, but as he had expected when he passed along the alley on one side of the Spanish Girl, a lamp was still burning inside a room at the back which he knew to be one which Jago used as an office.

By the time Orford rapped on the door

he had already assembled in his mind the small catalogue of points that he wished to make, and the very fact that he had come here to make them to Ranse Jago himself was a significant act in itself, but one that a less brash individual might have considered for somewhat longer and much more carefully than it seemed Orford had done.

At first surprise, even astonishment, struck dumb the big, heavy-faced man in shirtsleeves and with a cigar between his teeth, who admitted the Argon lawman. They stood facing one another, Jago bulky, Orford long and lean with his Adam's apple working, and if the new Argon sheriff felt, at the ultimate moment, even the merest doubt as to the wisdom of this bold approach, he was not deterred but plunged on into the substance of his business; and as Jago slowly removed the cigar from his mouth and stood staring at him, Orford, in his rather piping voice, traversed the situation of the town of Argon, the gravity of the task which had fallen to him, his perceived expectations of the townspeople in the matter, the fact that for the time being at least, he was compelled to act alone, there being no deputy in prospect, and coming nearer to the real reason for his being here at all, the concerns that were abroad about recent violent acts involving attacks on peaceful citizens. And then he came right out and mentioned Culp and Mellish, both of whom were known to be employees of Jago.

If Jago himself had lately had some doubts as to the wisdom of leaning on Charles Redwine as heavily as his men had done, spurred by a zeal to find out more about Gates and possibly discredit him, these hesitations were swamped by the surge of anger he now felt at the temerity of this jumped-up boy with a star pinned to his shirt, in linking him, Jago, with what had happened, and probably what had happened to Gates as well, and then having the brass nerve to belly up to him about it on his own premises. When he could speak, Jago said, 'Are yuh here to claim it was me roughed up Charlie Redwine?'

That was not what Orford had said at all and he now blinked and began to say, 'Not you in person—'

'Then are yuh here to say it was me that sent men a-purpose to do it? That it?'

'Mebbe not *sent*—'

'What in the name o' God *are* you sayin' then?'

'Mr Redwine, he got knocked around pretty bad.'

'Yeah? So did he come down an' complain about it? That what Charlie Redwine done?'

'No, not to me—'

'Well, did he give out to anybody else who it was that come an' did that to him?'

'No, Mr Redwine never did say...'

'But *you* say! An' what you say is that it was two men that's on my payroll, so how is it yuh know that, sheriff? Was yuh *there?*'

'No...' The folly of his coming here in the flush of his authority was now becoming manifestly clear to Orford, but of course it was much too late. 'But somebody did it.'

'An' if nobody else is sayin', even Redwine, what *you're* sayin' is it's got to be my boys.'

Floundering badly now, Orford said, 'Well, they been in nearly all o' the fights that there's been around Argon in some while, them two, an' that's well known.'

'Did that bastard Gates put yuh up to this? That found-out marshal from Wyomin' or wherever?'

If Orford paused to consider the question and knew that Gates' history had only surfaced in Argon after Redwine had been beaten, he now chose not to make an issue of it. What had seemed so telling a case when he had walked in here had been so swiftly demolished by this hard, overbearing man, on his own ground, that Orford was now effectively disarmed and certainly confused. The badge ought to have been more powerful than this.

'I ain't talked with Gates,' was all Orford could say.

'No? Well, I wouldn't be surprised if he didn't go crawlin' away ag'in like he crawled away from Laramie, an' now I'll tell yuh somethin' else that likely the people yuh *do* talk with ain't told yuh. That Gates bastard was here in Argon an' he got the jump on one o' my boys—them that yuh claim to be concerned about—an' he bust Culp's face, an' what I'm doin' now, fer Culp ain't feelin' so good, is layin' a complaint, an' it's ag'in Dave Gates. So, come mornin', what you're gonna do is git your ass right out there to that dirt farmer's outfit an' put some o' them questions to *him.* That all clear?' When Orford failed to open his mouth, Jago went on, fronting him, large chest almost touching him, and Jago actually tapped him with thick fingers that were still holding the cigar, the smoke from it causing Orford's eyes to smart and water. 'An' now yuh can do some listenin' to me, yuh fast-talkin', wet-eared little prick. Strut that star up an' down Main all yuh want, but come near me ag'in unless I send for yuh, or come near my boys with that accusin' mouth o' yourn an' I'll make sure it gits broke up with a pick-handle.' He gave the sacred badge of office on Orford's shirt a tweak. 'This thing ain't worth a shit 'til it's worn by a man, one like Restall. I got some plans in this region, sonny, an' they don't include some whinin' two-bit star-carrier with a fancy hat. Remember that an' you an' me, we'll rub along fine. Now git your ass out o' my place an' keep it out, an' when yuh see Gates, fetch the bastard back into Argon an' when yuh done that, send me word. But see it gits done.' A powerful hand dropped onto Orford's shoulder and with a fierce strength spun him around then shoved him abruptly across the room. 'Shut the door real quiet once you're through it.'

Charles Redwine was not at rest either, alone in his office, a bottle before him, already clouded with drink, his mind restless though, offering him no convenient escape into sleep; and it was not his still aching body and his still swollen face which was holding rest at bay. The demons were here again, in the shadows just beyond the reach of the solitary, low-turned lamp, the phantoms of past hurts and past failures, of personal weakness recurrently exposed in this town or that, the out-of-focus places and people of the past, with all their humiliations.

The brutal handling he had suffered at the hands of Jago's men had wounded his spirit even more than his physical self and it had required a monumental effort of will to try to conceal that truth from Gates. That act itself had perhaps been an attempt to redeem himself, to regain at least some scraps of his self-respect. But after Gates had gone, all of the old doubts and fears had come tumbling in on him, and though at first, as he always did, he had resisted reaching for the tempting bottle, he had succumbed, as he always did, and now was in that dangerous half-world between escape and oblivion and nagging awareness, a state in which at some stage he seemed to be standing off, studying objectively this hapless, pitiful man with flushed, veined face, clothing stained with spilled liquor, his breath foul, a travesty of a professional man living his desperate days behind a pathetic façade of good manners and studied speech, fearful of glancing behind him in the street lest he actually catch sight of reality, the disapproving, amused, pitying, scornful, disdainful faces looking at him after he had gone walking by.

A fire-line of neat whiskey went coursing slowly through him, causing him to gasp. He set the glass down vowing not to refill it. The low-burning lamp flickered. Redwine drew open a desk drawer and sat blinking down at the old army pistol, long barrelled and with an almost artistically curved butt of polished walnut, nearly beautiful and unquestionably deadly, heavy, with a slick-oiled look, the unlikely possession which in one past town or other he had been persuaded to acquire for his own protection. *'My God,'* thought Redwine, *'protection.'* Sometimes when alone like this he had lifted it, felt its seductive, solid weight, but on only a few occasions, and he had been quite serious when he had said to Gates, *'I've owned this for years but never even tried to use it.'* And Gates had been serious, too, and no doubt right when he had said, *'Whether it's loaded or not, if you'd tried for it, Charlie, they'd have killed you.'* Now Redwine made himself take up the pistol. He fumbled with it, snapped the cylinder out, then laid the big weapon on the desk. From a waxboard pack in the drawer he took six big .44, faintly grease-slick, bright brass loads with their ugly lead snouts. Awkwardly he pressed one after another in the cylinder, then snapped it home. As soon as he had done it he realized he did not know what had prompted him to load the pistol. He hefted it in his hand, freshly aware of the power of the great weapon, the ability it now possessed to maim, to take life, to alter the course of lives. Had he loaded it with the intention of destroying himself? If he had, then why six of the slick, fat bullets? Had he loaded it with some befuddled notion of taking revenge? If so, upon whom? Culp? Mellish? Jago? For those men had been Jago's creatures, come to him at Jago's behest. With a shudder Redwine put the pistol and the waxboard pack back in the drawer and slammed it shut. With waves of shame coming over him he shut his eyes

135

tightly and rested his head against the back of the chair as though the act of closing his eyes might somehow put all of the shadow-dwelling demons to flight and set him free. He drifted into a spinning darkness, then eventually into a deeply-breathing sleep.

With one boot Jago savagely slammed shut the door of a cupboard. Still in the office at the rear of the saloon he uncorked a bottle and slopped whiskey into a shot-glass and tossed back the drink, still red-faced with fury at the naive and cheeky visit he had had from Orford. Well, he had sorted that little bastard out and in a few hours he would do the same to Gates.

In the Lanyon house Stella Freeman lay sleepless in her bed, more disturbed by the events which, it seemed, were now to take Dave Gates away from the vicinity of Argon than she had been prepared to admit, even to herself. And the covert discussions in the town—and even more open ones in some quarters—now that Gates' history was common knowledge, meant that should he come into Argon again, those who earlier had been well-disposed towards him might now choose to turn away. Much of that, she thought, would be some absurd taking of moral high ground which, as she herself had come to know, would be indefensible. Plenty of folk in the town would not relish having their own past lives opened to public scrutiny. But that would probably make no difference.

Inside the Argon Bank and Loan, Quint, hat over his face, was stretched out and rumbling steadily. Reeby, nearby, almost asleep, started up at a small sound, then after a few seconds of peering into the swimming dimness, saw that the noise had been made by Pearsall who was now sitting propped against the door of the vault and was loading his shotgun.

In a bitingly cold camp outside Argon, near the picketed, sometimes shifting horses, Sears lay under the blankets in an almost foetal position, trying to induce sleep that might overcome the throbbing pain in his side. Just beyond him Sears could see the rise of the brush, brush that almost rimmed the camp-site, sketched faintly against the moonless sky, a slight breeze moving skeletal branches, making fleeting shapes as in some sombre *danse macabre,* perhaps an eerie prelude to events in the morning to come.

ELEVEN

Neatly turned out in a suit, as he was required to be, young Jay Lanyon came along the boardwalk, heading to work, the bank now within his sight and the time almost eight twenty-five.

The new day was less cloudy than the night had been, but from time to time a slight breeze lifted spins of dust along the streets.

In his musty office, Charles Redwine struggled to free himself from a reeking pit of agony, his limbs stiffened from hours slumped in his chair sleeping, his head fit to burst with the pulsing drumbeats which were the aftermath of his heavy drinking. A wave of sweating nausea swept over him and he was compelled to sit quite still, drawing in deep breaths, releasing them gradually, swallowing frequently, until the spasming impulse to vomit was suppressed. Almost ten minutes passed before Redwine trusted himself sufficiently to get to his feet, and once he had achieved that, he made his way carefully to a cupboard from which he carried back to his desk two bottles, one of port wine and one of French brandy. He then fetched a tumbler and proceeded to mix a drink of wine and brandy, and then without pausing to dwell on it, quickly drank down the vile-tasting concoction after which he put the empty glass down and leaned the heels of his hands on the edge of the desk and stood quite still. Presently Redwine emitted an enormous belch, breathed deeply several times and then straightened up, feeling much restored. He scraped long fingers at stubble around his jaw and glanced down at his stained and rumpled clothing. He thought he might clear away the bottles and glasses, then perhaps sit gathering himself for a short while before making his way back to the rooming-house where he lived, to take a hot tub and get fresh clothing.

Stripped to the waist, standing in his private room at the Spanish Girl, Jago was sluicing water from a large white bowl over his head and shoulders, having lately finished shaving. Before this day was much further advanced he intended to go along Main to make quite sure that Matt Orford had taken seriously what had been said to him and had gone out there to fetch Gates back into Argon.

James Fleury, approaching the bank from the opposite direction, his small eyeglasses glinting, would arrive at the front door, he noted, at about the same time as young Jay Lanyon who, having paused for a word or two with Pauling who had been in the act of unlocking his shop, was now coming near the bank. Out of long habit Fleury fingered a silver watch from a vest pocket and snapped it open, then shut it and put it away. Almost eight-thirty.

Along the street a couple of freight-wagons were moving slowly, their big wheels lifting powdery dust, and one or two people were to be seen along the boardwalks; and a swamper, having emerged from one of the saloons, steaming pail in hand, pitched the contents into the street.

To Lanyon's 'Good morning, Mr Fleury,' the man with the eyeglasses merely nodded curtly, produced a ring of keys from a pocket of his black jacket, stepped to the door and inserted a key. When he pushed the stout door open he made a quick motion with his head for Lanyon to go in first. Fleury followed him in and closed the door behind him, turning an inside latch to secure it again, an unvarying ritual through all his years of senior service at the Bank and Loan.

Lanyon and Fleury had progressed halfway up the room beyond the main counters, moving between empty desks and chairs, when Quint, great pistol in hand, emerged from early-morning shadows in a place whose shades were still drawn over the few barred windows this building possessed.

Face whitening, Jay Lanyon stopped abruptly, Fleury too, but Fleury had to put one hand on one of the desks to steady himself; and before he had even begun to recover from the initial shock of Quint, Reeby appeared, and Pearsall in the long coat and carrying the fearsome, two-barrelled shotgun.

Fleury got as far as saying, 'What—?' But Quint chopped him off real quick.

'Shut your womany little mouth. Jes' nod or shake your head. You the one that opens that can o' money over there?'

Fleury licked his lips and nodded jerkily.

To Pearsall, Reeby muttered, 'That's five to me.' Pearsall merely grunted.

Lanyon made the safest choice he could possibly have made, he stood utterly still. Fleury, his face ashen, was beginning to sweat and to tremble slightly. He was utterly appalled. These filthy men with their soiled and dusty clothing *stank:* their breaths, their bodies and everything they were wearing stank foully. Unshaven and with wind-reddened eyes they were all that a bank clerk's nightmares were made of, and here they were, early in the morning, incomprehensibly *inside* the Argon bank. Fleury's flick of a glance at the clock above the door of the vault, now showing eight thirty-seven, was not missed by Quint.

'Don't go frettin about what time it is,' Quint said. 'Jes' git them keys an' git this here door open an' find some sacks for the carryin' away.'

Fleury moved forward and with fingers that were curiously stiff, began sorting through the keys on the steel ring, and motioning to Lanyon said, as though summoning some shreds of his authority in this place, 'Canvas sacks, Mr Lanyon.' He might have been calling the young man up to attend to the needs of a customer.

Lanyon went across to a cupboard, Reeby tracking him and watching closely as Lanyon produced several white canvas sacks about twelve inches by eighteen, the

143

bank's name imprinted on them in black, and all with cord drawstrings threaded through them.

Pearsall, seeing all this activity under way, went wandering around, the shotgun now under one arm, poking and prying here and there now that there was sufficient light to see by.

'Hurry it up,' Quint said, coughing and giving Fleury a shove.

'I am doing this as quickly as I can,' Fleury said almost brusquely, at which response Quint, half spinning his body, caught the man a savage back-hander across the face, sending him thumping down to the floor. The key was already in the lock of the vault. Quint motioned with his head to Lanyon.

'You do it, boy, an' don't go back-answerin' as well, or I'll bust your ass.'

Fleury, lower lip bleeding, was now scratching around on the floor trying to find his eyeglasses as Lanyon went to the door of the vault, turned the key stiffly and pulled the solid-feeling door open.

'There's a lamp inside,' Lanyon said.

To Reeby, Quint said, 'Light it,' and Reeby stepped forward, led the way in and struck a match. To Lanyon, Quint said, 'Fetch them bags in here pronto, boy.'

When Reeby, Lanyon and Quint were all inside the dimly-lit brick vault, Fleury, having recovered his eyeglases, fortunately undamaged, put them on, and then he did what neither his nature nor his punctilious training could ever have suggested he might do. He made a run for it.

Clattering against chairs, knocking one over, bruising a leg on the corner of a desk, Fleury went careering up beyond the brass-trimmed counters to the front door where he scrabbled at the latch, and in a lather of haste, flung the door wide open.

At that instant the long-coated figure of Pearsall appeared seemingly out of nowhere and came charging after the bank man, shotgun in hand, just as James Fleury was framed in the outer brightness of the open doorway. The deep clap of the shotgun assailed the ears of all who were inside the bank, blue smoke came leaping, and bits of wadding, and the sound of the bunched shot striking Fleury was a heavy *whack* and it was as though he had been picked up by some invisible hand and hurled outside, and by the time his body, executing an obscene, ragged, bloody pirouette had reached the boardwalk, Pearsall was at the door letting blast the second barrel, catching Fleury again, blood spraying from him, the riven body, clothing rent asunder, cast, clumping heavily, onto the dusty street like some discarded bolster.

Pearsall calmly broke open the shotgun and began the process of removing discharged cartridges and inserting fresh ones. It was now eight thirty-four. Pearsall turned his head and called to Quint who had come out of the vault, 'Had to do it. The little bastard was near to bein' away.'

What Quint thought about this development was unclear, for he did not answer Pearsall but instead called to Lanyon,

'C'mon boy, move your ass fillin' them sacks!'

But Reeby said, 'The fat's in the fire now, Quinney.'

Quint looked up at the clock. Almost eight thirty-five. Sears was not due until eight forty-five.

Out beyond the town, Sears, greasy with sweat, had almost completed a stiff, agonizing saddling of the horses and in fact was bending to the last of the cinches when his ear caught the distant, dull thumps from the direction of Argon and with difficulty he straightened and for a few moments supported himself against the horse. His wound was now much worse and he felt it, and if his ears had not deceived him something unplanned had happened.

At his window overlooking Main, Redwine recoiled in horror as he witnessed the brutal shotgun killing of James Fleury, and whoever else happened to be on the street at that same moment and within sight of it seemed to have become frozen in their disbelief before there occurred a general scattering for cover.

Afterwards Redwine did not recall in detail what he had done then; but when he went lurching and clumping down the outside stairway he had in one hand the loaded, heavy pistol but no idea whatsoever what had prompted him to bring it, and certainly no notion of what he might expect to do with it.

Jago, striding through the damp-smelling long room that formed the main part of the saloon, between tables with chairs still lifted up on them off the swabbed floor, was suddenly confronted by the swamper, eyes dilated in his pudding face, pointing towards the street.

'He's shot, Mr Jago! He's shot down!'

'Who? Who's shot?'

'Feller that come out o' the bank! That Fleury.'

Jago stopped. He was carrying no weapon. Quickly he went around the long bar and returned with a large Colt pistol, bellowing for Mellish and for Culp, both of whom lived on the premises. Already dressed, they had heard the shotgun and appeared almost immediately, Culp still showing swollen evidence of his encounter with Gates.

'It's all on at the bank,' Jago said. 'Jim Fleury's shot.'

So it transpired that Mellish, Culp and Jago appeared out in front of the Spanish Girl about the same time as Redwine came onto Main, all looking and then moving towards the fallen Fleury, Redwine in his sharp way noticing that though bandits were apparently inside the bank, not a single horse was standing at the hitching-rail over there, and his mind moved on to the assumption that the horses must therefore be around the back of the building.

As it happened, Mellish and Culp, jogging, were the first to arrive at the spot where Fleury lay, and even though Jago, following more watchfully, called a sharp warning, were suddenly under blasting gunfire, not from a shotgun but a pistol, this in the hand of Quint who had just then come up to the doorway to have a look around.

Lead whacked into Mellish, his hat fell off and he sat down abruptly and began coughing blood; and Culp, though bringing his own pistol up fast, also fell, crying out, clutching at his lower stomach. Jago then fired but the fierce apparition that had been Quint had by then vanished. Mellish fell sideways, quivering, then after a kind of stretching motion, lay still. Culp, in his loud agony, in a kind of slow motion, was trying to move himself away from the lethal doorway but not managing to get very far.

In a common unspoken purpose, Jago and Redwine, dangerously exposed, came together over the sorely-wounded Culp, both of whose hands were now pressed firmly into his groin and who was clearly losing a lot of blood and in great pain. 'I've got this arm, take the other,' Redwine said. Jago did so and in this way they conveyed Culp, his toes dragging, raising fine dust, towards the opposite side of the street, their backs to the bank and therefore to whoever might again appear there, shooting. Redwine could feel an odd tingling sensation in his neck and at the backs of his knees, anticipating God knew what at any instant. *'Let it be a clean kill, not a crippling wound...'* But there had been not the merest hesitation on Redwine's part. He had not stopped to reflect upon who it was who was down, wounded, except that it was another man, one of three that had been hit, the others plainly beyond anybody's help.

The calls that had gone up and the loud shooting, cries of *'Jim Fleury's shot!'* had soon swept the main street of Argon clean of people, and any who had been emerging, asking what the hell was going on, were soon enough waved back in again.

But one man—who had been preparing to go down to the bank a little later—and who was greatly alarmed and would not be deflected from his purpose in finding out what was happening, was the banker himself, the tubby little man Brophy. Somewhat querulously, not as completely attired as usual, he now appeared on Main, and when Jago, who was by this time in the doorway of the Spanish Girl—to which place the sorely injured Culp had been taken—called loudly to him to get himself to safety, he hesitated as Jago bawled, 'Fleury's dead! Yuh can't do nothin' fer him, nor Mellish. An' Culp's hit real bad. Yuh want to do somethin', go fetch Doc Brill here, by the back way.' If Brophy was unaccustomed to being spoken to in such a peremptory manner he did not now take exception to it, but withdrew, presumably to do as Jago wanted.

Redwine now moved on past Jago who wanted to know where he was going.

'Around the back of the bank,' Redwine said. 'Whoever they are, their horses have to be there. While you're here they can't come out front without getting shot at. I might be able to do something when they come out the back.' Then he said, 'We'll need to take care though. Young Lanyon must be in that bank; he generally arrives with Jim Fleury.' And he had to say, 'If we can just keep them inside there, maybe we should get some more help.' For some reason he did not even mention

Orford. 'Maybe we should send for Dave Gates.'

'The hell with that bastard!' snapped Jago.

Redwine shrugged and left, angling across the street, keeping an eye on the door of the bank until some such time as his progress effectively hid him from the direct view of anyone there. But Redwine was feeling much less confident now, for he had had time to think. Oddly the two men in Argon who might have made the difference in something like this, Culp and Mellish, were out of it. And Redwine was at last beginning to wonder where the Argon sheriff could possibly be.

Jago, mulling over that same question, had just concluded that it did now seem likely that the boy had actually done as he had been told to do and had already left for the Gates homestead.

Around on the back street, moving with caution, the unfamiliar weapon heavy in his hand, Charles Redwine was surprised to see no sign of horses there either.

TWELVE

Gates swung the axe, driving it hard into the block and leaving it there. Knuckles on hips he then stood staring up at the mounted man.

'I don't believe I'm hearing this right, Orford.'

Orford was sitting the sleek black horse, stroking its neck with one gloved hand, blinking down at Gates, not quite as sure of himself now, for clearly it was not to be as straightforward a matter as he had envisaged.

'It's, uh, well it's jes' that there's been this here complaint.'

'From Ranse Jago, you say?'

'Yeah, Mr Jago, he was real set on it, on account o' his man, Culp.'

'An' you have to do whatever Jago tells you to do. Is that it?'

Orford looked away, then back at Gates.

'It ain't that. When I git a complaint I got to foller it up. Anyway, that's what Mr Restall done, regular, follered up complaints.'

'I know what Mr Restall did,' Gates said. 'Mr Restall made a point of following up all the complaints that made sense. That's the difference.' He was now beginning to wonder how far Orford was prepared to push this, which meant, in all likelihood, by how much Ranse Jago had got him bluffed. So he asked, 'What if I refuse to go?'

Orford was blinking rapidly again, a faint flush coming into his thin, sallow face. Gates watched him for a few seconds longer then turned away as though he might be dismissing the entire matter. Almost in disbelief he heard the ratchety clicking of a pistol being cocked.

'We got to go now,' Orford said.

Well, that answered the question about Jago's influence over this boy badge-carrier. Gates turned slowly to face the mounted man again, this time looking into the great black eye of Orford's pistol. Now that Orford had gone as far as drawing the weapon, this affair had moved to a different level, and while Gates gave him a look of outright contempt, he also realized, for he had come across the likes of Orford in the past, that a man with such nervous eyes was highly dangerous when holding a loaded and cocked firearm, more dangerous in some circumstances than a man who had drawn in anger. Gates knew, also, that the drawing of the gun had another significance, even though he himself was unarmed, for Orford would know by now that he was by no means confronting some ordinary sodbuster, disturbed at the ploughing, but a man who, in his time, had carried a badge and the means to back it up, and by all accounts had walked through his share of gunsmoke, even if his career as a peacekeeper had ended dubiously in a bright sundown in Laramie.

That was most likely why Orford then chose to dismount carefully and hitch his black horse to the rail of the porch and why thereafter he tracked Gates closely, never taking his jumpy eyes off him, while Gates fetched the mare and set about hitching her to his wagon.

Gates did say, when he had done this, 'No good will come of this, Orford, you can be sure of that.'

'I got no choice,' Orford said, 'I got to do it.'

'Yeah,' said Gates, 'every puppet has to when his strings get pulled.'

Moving among a miscellany of shacks and lean-to's, pausing then near a corral behind one of the town liveries, Redwine had by now become convinced that, there being no saddled horses behind the bank, none was concealed nearby, either. Neither was there any sign of human movement at the back door of the place, which in fact looked to be securely shut. Redwine was still trying to get to grips with this when he believed that his ear had caught the sound of horses on the move. Redwine turned at that sound and retraced his steps, the ache in his head, which had to some extent receded, now coming back with a dull insistence. What he badly needed was a drink. When he again went walking along beside the livery corral he saw that just out beyond the town by about a hundred yards, but coming closer, was a single mounted man sitting his saddle oddly, as though hurt in some way, and leading by means of lines attached to his saddle-horn, two left, one right, three other saddled horses.

The instant that Redwine got a look at this unusual sight he realized what was happening; these were the mounts belonging to whoever was inside the bank. In getting a clearer view of them Redwine had slowly moved out a short distance from the corral, so that at about the same time that the attorney saw the advancing rider, the rider saw Redwine observing him and at once began slowing his advance; but he had something of a handful out there and what he was now doing caused the led horses to react somewhat, and when they all finally came to a halt they were whickering and tossing their heads, manes flashing in the morning light, stepping and screwing sideways.

Redwine, suddenly alarmed at being

alone, stepped back close to the long, warped poles of the corral and in an act of nervous defensiveness, laid his right arm along one of them, aiming the long military pistol more or less in the direction of the curiously crouching horseman.

The thunderclap of the shot bucked the pistol upwards, wafted acrid smoke all around Redwine's head and caused the man with the horses to begin working urgently at getting his jittery entourage on the move again and wheeling away.

Redwine glanced around and was surprised to see the angular-looking man, Pauling, in his white shop-apron, coming uncertainly towards him. It did appear that, incomprehensibly, Pauling did not intend sitting on the fence in this affair.

Out in the rough, dusty country Sears, yapping and urging his charges, had now got them turning and was heading away back towards brush-studded, rocky cover. Ordinarily Sears might have pressed on towards the bank no matter what, but he was wounded and sick and somewhat confused. Redwine did consider shooting at him again, then didn't go on with it, and when Pauling came nervously closer, said, 'Now, whoever they are, they're trapped inside the bank; but so is Jay Lanyon.'

Inside the bank, Quint once again had approached the front door and began yelling to anyone who would listen, 'Keep clear! We got a bank man in here! Keep clear or I'll blow one in his mouth!'

Eventually it was Jago's heavy voice that answered from across the street. 'Yuh been heard!'

Then, from some distance away there was the sound of a gunshot and for a while nobody heard any more from inside the bank. In fact not much else seemed to be happening until, near the end of the main street a skinny man wearing a white apron appeared, waving his arms until Jago, in the doorway of his saloon, gave a brief hand-motion of acknowledgement. Pauling made pointing gestures in the general direction of Redwine's disappearance and Jago beckoned to the shop-keeper but also made a slow circling motion with his arm, for he thought that Pauling might have been just stupid enough to come blundering along Main and so risk getting himself shot.

In the saloon behind Jago, Doc Brill, narrow faced, with his thick white eyebrows and thick white hair, said, 'Your man's not in good shape at all, Ranse. I've got the bleeding held up but I can't do much more; and it might not be enough. The bullet went through but it made one hell of a mess of him. I've given him something to dull the pain. Once he's settled some, I'll have another look, but I have to say I'm not hopeful.'

Jago did not turn his head but nodded, and then he said, 'They're gonna use young Lanyon to bargain with, I reckon.' And, 'Charlie Redwine's gone around the back an' it sounded like he let 'em know he's there.'

The doctor grunted and then asked, 'Where the hell's the new lawman?'

Jago shrugged. 'Could be he's gone out of Argon fer a time.'

Brill stared at the back of Jago's head but did not pursue the matter. Brill did not much like Jago, but in circumstances such as these, divisions tended to disappear, at least temporarily, and unlikely alliances might be formed. Instead, Brill said, 'Bess Lanyon is in some kind of state, of course, about her boy being in there, and Bob's had to be talked out of trying to approach the bank, but that niece of theirs, Miss Freeman, she's a level-headed lady if ever I saw one, and she's talking some sense into the pair of them.' Brill sighed. 'Sometimes it takes adversity to find out just where the strong people are. My God, Ranse, this is a damn' mess and no mistake.'

For a moment the mention of Stella Freeman had distracted Jago but now he came back to immediate matters and looked for further signs of Pauling but there were none. Hardly had Jago done this, however, than the swamper, somewhere in the dimmer recesses of the saloon, said, 'Mr Jago?'

When Jago stepped back in through the batwing doors, squinting in the interior gloom, he saw that Pauling had in fact arrived.

'I've just talked with Charlie Redwine,' Pauling said. His voice was cracking but at least he was here. 'They're trapped over there in that bank. There was a man fetching horses in but Charlie fired at him an' turned him around an' drove him off. So they got no horses.'

'They've got young Jay Lanyon though,' Doc Brill said with some asperity, 'so in the finish, what they want, they'll get.'

Echoing Brill, Jago muttered, 'Jesus, what a mess.'

'On the way here,' said Pauling, 'I talked with Brophy. He's wanting to know where Matt Orford is. He's heard he's not down at the jailhouse an' nobody seems to have seen him this morning.'

'We should all like to know where Matt Orford's got to,' said Brill rather primly. Then, 'Whatever we do we can't have young Jay Lanyon put in any more danger. These men are mad dogs.'

Jago stepped again to the batwing doors and stood staring out at the street. The bodies of Fleury and Mellish lay under whirling clouds of flies and with powdery dust blown against them and over them. Accepting what Brill had been saying, for it must surely be the reality of the situation, Jago said, 'Yeah, we'll likely have to trade their horses for Lanyon, if we kin git hold of the horses.' He stepped through the batwings and onto the boardwalk and bellowed 'Bank!' Nobody else seemed to be taking the initiative so Jago had resolved to get hold of the matter. How still the town lay in this warm, slightly windy morning, how abandoned. Jago waited, listening for some response from across the street.

Still near the corral, Redwine was now in a most uncertain frame of mind, feeling a long way out of his depth, recent events having occurred in the flush of blind urgency and in self-defence and involving others as well as Redwine himself. As far as the attorney was concerned the actions he had taken so far were completely foreign to his nature. He was simply not a violent man though he had personally suffered violence and had even been the subject of contempt. No, all this striding about with pistols was not Charles Redwine. Without pausing for rational thought he had set himself against men to whom violence was second nature and to whom human life meant nothing.

The man and the saddled horses had passed from Redwine's view among rocks and brush and even the considerable dust they had been raising had now been wind-blown to nothing. It did now occur to Redwine that if he were to continue to stand his ground here, watching the back of the bank as he had told Jago he would do, then it would have been preferable, almost, to have had that horseman coming even closer to where he was and shooting at him, rather than vanishing from sight; for now there was the awful possibility that when that man returned—and Redwine was quite convinced that he would—it was most likely that, having been shot at once, he would make the next approach with studied caution, slipping up, if he could, on Redwine; and in that sort of activity, Redwine knew with a stomach-churning certainty that he would not stand a chance.

The luck he had had so far could never hold. Now, wiping at his sweating face, eyes stinging from blown dust, he must do his best to watch all ways at once while still not neglecting his chief surveillance of the bank.

Redwine's breathing was not yet under control from all his exertions and he knew that if by some means he should survive the next half-hour he would then be impelled to review all of the things he had done so unthinkingly between the moment he had seen Fleury killed and the moment he had discharged this old military pistol at a mounted man he had never encountered before in his life: the blundering descent of the outside stairs, the unbelievable if unspoken alliance with Ranse Jago, the appalling risks he had taken for the sake of another man who not long ago had been a party to savagely beating him. Redwine, the breeze tugging at his clothing, his head aching, waited.

Jago lifted his head slightly. He partly raised the big Colt he was holding. Somebody was across there near to the front doorway of the bank, for there had been a brief shadow cast by movement. Jago shouted, 'Your mounts can't git near! We drove your man off! We'll let 'em through when yuh let the boy go!'

If this had been heard and properly understood it drew no response and no-one stepped into view at the bank. As a precaution Jago raised his pistol, lining up on the doorway opposite.

Inside that place Reeby was busy making sure that the drawstrings on all of the now filled canvas sacks were pulled tight and well secured; and he had found sufficient spare lengths of cord to provide the means of lashing them all to the horses when the time came, for there would not be enough room in the saddlebags. That was an operation, however, which would require several minutes, some patience and consequently some security from attack.

Quint came pacing down the room between the desks and chairs, his spurs on and clinking as he walked, drawn pistol hanging at his side, his inflamed eyes blinking, his expression unreadable but his mind no doubt active.

Pearsall was standing with the twin barrels of his shotgun across one of Lanyon's narrow shoulders. To Lanyon, Quint now said, 'Yuh hear all that out there?'

'Yes,' said Lanyon, for otherwise there had been a deep silence and his mind, sharpened by fear, had been ready to receive any word from out there which might provide some evidence that his plight was known about and that there were people who were deeply concerned for his safety. But all of that did not alter one whit the truly appalling fact that James Fleury, who could have done nothing to them by running away, had simply been shot down like some diseased animal and that the foul-smelling man who had done it was right now standing at his own back.

'Whose was that real big mouth over yonder? Was that your banker?'

'No, that wasn't Mr Brophy. It sounded more like the man who runs the saloon across there, Ranse Jago.' Lanyon's voice was almost cracking, for now that the practical activity of filling the sacks was over, he could not rid himself of the sight and sound of Fleury being blasted to death from the doorway—and the fact that as he had been speaking, the shotgun resting on his shoulder had moved slightly—and that somebody else out there, he did not know who, had been shot dead by this man with the pistol, and a third man had been wounded. It was like some dreadful nightmare; and suddenly it came into Lanyon's mind that he could not yet believe he would never again see James Fleury in this place, wearing his odd little eyeglasses and hear his fussy voice: *'Look sharp, Mr Lanyon. Can you not see there are customers waiting?'* The young man's head sank down as, unexpectedly, he felt an awful, empty sadness that this should have come to pass. He was jerked back to the reality of it, however, when Quint said to Reeby, 'When yuh finished that, go take a look out back.'

Pearsall said, 'Yuh reckon that prick was bluffin'?'

'We'll know when we git a look.

Somebody out back there shot at somethin' an' we sure ain't heard nothin' from Sears.'

Sears in fact was in a great deal of pain, his entire left side seeming to be alive with relentlessly throbbing fires, but he was compelling himself to remain on his feet just long enough to take out whoever that bastard was near the corral, the one that had taken a shot at him; and then to get all their horses down to that bank as he was supposed to do. Something must have gone badly wrong but whatever it was they must still have plenty of fire-power and there had been no sounds of general shooting in the town, no suggestion whatever of the bank being rushed. Screened by brush he had managed to get all the horses picketed and settled down and he was now coming in, albeit slowly and painfully, and screened as much as possible by brush, on foot. And there, behind the livery building, was the corral.

The elder Lanyons, their faces ravaged, seeming shrunken in their anxiety, had slowly come to accept the fact that there was nothing that they personally could do. It was far from clear, however, particularly to Bob Lanyon, precisely who *was* doing something, and what.

'Where's that Matt Orford?' he wanted to know and not for the first time since this affair began. 'I've not seen a whisker of Orford. Has anybody?'

Stella Freeman, looking strained but still well in control of herself and the domestic situation in this time of dire crisis, shook her head. When the first startled cry had gone up and the word had swept swiftly through Argon and there had been the sudden sounds of shooting somewhere, Stella had been in the act of putting her hair up preparatory to leaving to take classes at the Argon schoolhouse. That preliminary task had not been done and consequently her rich brown hair was still loose, reaching halfway down her slim back; but right now that seemed not to have the slightest importance.

'When I went out front earlier,' she said, 'though I didn't go as far as Main, I did hear it said that nobody had been able to find Matt Orford.' She did not say it to the Lanyons but she wished sincerely that Dave Gates had been on hand. When all had been said and done, the greatest fear that she had, based on what she knew of the events that had taken place along Main, was that Ranse Jago, incensed by the killing of his employee, playing the big man, the self-styled strong man of Argon, might somehow enlist enough support for an all-out assault on the bank, and if that were to happen, more lives might be lost and perhaps among them, Jay Lanyon's. She said, 'I can't just stay here. I've simply got to find out what's happening, who's doing something. But promise me the both of you, that you'll wait in this house 'til I get back. I'll try not to be long.'

Bess's tear-damp face was pleading. 'You can't go out, Stella. That's madness.'

'I don't intend going anywhere near the bank,' Stella said, 'but surely some of the men in Argon can tell me how matters stand now. Doctor Brill, perhaps.' And again, 'I'll not be long.' Before either of them could voice any further protest she had slipped from the room.

At the livery corral, Sears, dusty, soaked in sweat and bludgeoned with pain, propped himself against one of the corner poles and slowly drew down on Redwine.

THIRTEEN

Something, though he knew not what, told Redwine that he was in mortal danger, but by the time this realization came to him it was too late. The loud explosion of the pistol was coincident with the sledgehammer blow that thumped Redwine forward, executing a couple of almost comic steps before he was flung full on his face, losing hold of the army pistol, hit solidly in the left shoulder.

Gunsmoke was swimming around Sears as he clutched on to the corral pole, blinking his reddened eyes, trying to see whether or not there were any other men anywhere near this back street; but as far as he was able to establish, there were not, the blowing down of the pistol-man having attracted no other activity. Sears began to go awkwardly away again, heading back to the place where he had left the horses.

First numbed by the impact of the heavy slug, Redwine was now beginning to feel deep, throbbing pain such as he had never felt before, such pain and such a wave of sweating nausea that when first he tried to move he began to vomit, but all he was fetching up was stale liquor, and so sourly vile was it that it made him want to vomit the more. Rich blood was on the ground under him and dust was whipping over him, driven by the intermittent breeze. *'Oh, mother of God, send somebody to help me...'* Desperately, lest the man who had shot him now moved in to finish the job, Redwine began making almost maniacal efforts to roll onto his unwounded shoulder so that he could then try to inch himself along using one arm and one leg for leverage. Main, for that was where he was trying to go, seemed a very long way off.

Stella Freeman came to the corner of the street where stood a print shop and she risked a cautious look up and down Main, watching the dust going skimming along the street and seeing far down near the bank, two dark, unmoving shapes, like black stones cast there. She knew quite well that they would be the bodies of the dead men. No horses stood at hitching-rails. Nothing except the dust and a scrap or two of paper was moving on the entirety of the street. It was almost eerie.

Uncertain what she ought to do next, if anything, she stood wondering where Doc Brill might be at this moment; or anybody at all who might be able to give her some news of Jay Lanyon. She was just about to turn reluctantly and walk away, perhaps with some thought of trying to find Brill by making her way along a back street to the rear of Jago's place; when, along a side street directly opposite, she saw the alarming sight of a man crawling, or rather inching his way along the ground, and cast awkwardly over on one side. Not at first

175

able to see who it was because of distance and because of the dust blowing, she first took a careful look up Main and then, grey skirts in hand, her long brown hair blowing, she ran directly across the street to the shelter of a corner where stood a feed and grain on the one hand and on the opposite corner one of the Argon liveries.

She now thought she could recognize the crawling man. Surely it was Charles Redwine. Starting forward, a sound made her stop in her tracks and turn, and her pulses leaped when she saw, bowling along the trail into Argon, Dave Gates' flat-decked wagon drawn by the single mare; and jogging steadily, though somehow importantly alongside it, the much sought-after Argon peacekeeper, Matt Orford. At once Stella began motioning urgently for them to come right across into the sidestreet where she was.

They arrived, dust rising all around them as Gates hauled his wagon to a stop, and Orford reined in his dusty black. Stella pointed towards the now inert figure of Redwine and as they moved on again towards him, she tried to tell them the bare facts of all that had happened, as far as she knew them, and urged them to take care not to approach the Argon bank.

'They're in there. I don't know how many, but they're very dangerous. Two men dead, and one—I guess two now— wounded. I don't know why they're still inside the bank, but they are, and they're holding Jay Lanyon.'

Redwine knew though for when they got to him, Gates springing down off the wagon, Orford dismounting, Redwine's dusty, sweat-marked face managed to look up at them and it was hideous yet almost clown-like. And there was a lot of blood over Redwine's left side and back.

'They...held their horses off... I don't know why... Nobody saw them go into...the bank. I had...pistol...lost it.'

Gates asked Stella, 'Where's Doc Brill?'

Stella said, 'I don't know, but I think he did go down earlier to the Spanish Girl to attend to one of Jago's men.'

'We'll get Charlie up on the wagon,' Gates said, and to Orford who was now looking none too sure of himself, 'If I'm going to be any use at all, I'll need to be armed.'

They lifted Redwine onto the wagon as gently as they could, though he seemed to have slipped from consciousness, his head flopping over loosely.

'I'll fetch you George Restall's gun,' Orford said, and added in an almost excited tone, 'But jes' you remember, Gates, whatever happens, I'm the man in charge here.'

Gates had been preparing to climb up on the wagon but Stella touched his arm. 'I can do that, Dave. I have to do *something*. I'll drive it around behind Jago's and if the doc isn't still there, I'll find him. Mr Redwine needs help as soon as he can get it.'

After only a brief hesitation, Gates nodded. 'Go real careful, Stella.'

Stella Freeman climbed up on the wagon and lost no time in turning the rig around, and she had passed across Main, and Orford, remounted, had headed away to the jailhouse to fetch Restall's pistol when, just as Redwine had done, earlier, Gates heard the sound of horses approaching and turned to see, in the brushy country just out of Argon, dust rising around them, three led horses, a single, bent-over rider bringing them.

Gates had to weigh up his next move in a real hurry: retreat onto Main, allowing the horses to be brought in, or make some sort of attempt to prevent it. It seemed somehow unfair to Redwine, for one, not to do the latter. It was then that something that Redwine had said came back to him. *'I had...pistol...lost it.'* Lost it where? Near where he got hit, and by the looks of him Charlie had not come far, since.

Gates thereupon began jogging forward and though the wind-blown dust was already beginning to cover them, the drag-marks of Redwine's tortuous progress could still be discerned. They led Gates to where they had begun, the side of the corral.

The horses were coming closer and now there was a shout, probably to the horseman, from somewhere across to his left and a glance showed him the figure of a man framed in the bank's back doorway, indeed urging the horseman in. Quickly Gates cast about for the pistol; and then there it was, where it had fallen from Redwine's hand, the old U.S. Army weapon the attorney had had in his office.

Gates got it in his own hand fast and came up blasting, and for the second time that morning Sears, his vision now clouded not only by dust, but losing full awareness, such was his pain, made an attempt to slow the horses and wheel them away.

From the direction of the bank a gunshot blasted and dangerous lead came whispering, but Gates turned, arm scything down, and thundered a shot at the man along there, causing him to nip back instinctively to the cover of the doorway. Then Gates saw that the horses were coming on again, so he began tracking with the long pistol ahead of the oddly-swaying man bringing them, then let the thunderclap of the shot go, smelling the tangy smoke from the discharge.

Sears seemed to jump in the saddle, then in the blink of an eye he was gone from sight, down among the striking hooves, and the horses were all tossing and weaving and screwing around amid surging dust, and when they had more or less come to a halt, began trying to pull away from each other, the one to which the others were attached rearing and screaming. They were still some seventy yards short of the bank. To the now vanished shooter, Gates shouted, 'Come out an' get 'em!'

Inside the bank when Reeby came part of the way back from the door from which he had shot at a man up by the corral and had been shot at in return, he called, 'Sears looks to be done fer!'

'Where's the goddamn' mounts?' asked Quint loudly.

'Sears come down tryin' to git 'em here, an' the bastard that did it, he's still out there coverin' the back.'

'Are they all together still? How far out?'

'Yeah... Fifty yards... No, mebbe more.'

'They have to be got,' called Quint, 'an' got now.'

'I'll go do it,' Reeby said.

'Watch this one,' said Quint to Pearsall, for the man in the long coat had now moved away from Lanyon and was clearly angry, looking as though he would have liked to discharge his shotgun at something—anything.

'We oughta jes' blow this little bastard's head off,' Pearsall said.

'No, not yet, anyways,' Quint said. 'He's a card we'll likely have to play.'

Pearsall merely glowered at Lanyon, making no further comment.

Quint moved up towards the front door. All now depended on Reeby's getting hold of the horses. After that they would take their chances though he was fully aware that, in a general shoot, anything could happen. And now it seemed that Sears was dead. Idly, then, Quint puzzled over the fact that as far as he knew, the lawman in this town had not come to the fore, the man Quint now remembered as Crawford.

There had only been this Jago mouthing off. Then Quint swore savagely, for he suddenly remembered that Sears had got his watch.

To a face at a rear window of the Spanish Girl and without first climbing down off the wagon, Stella Freeman called, 'Doctor Brill?'

A man in an apron appeared in the doorway. 'He ain't here.'

Then further along at the back of a dry goods store the doctor appeared, and at his elbow Brophy of the bank, both in their shirtsleeves, the doctor's clothes showing smears of blood. Brill at once assessed what the woman was here for and waved her forward.

'There's a back room in here we can take him to.'

By the time they got Charles Redwine down off the wagon and inside, he was starting to come round.

'Matt Orford's back,' Stella said, 'and he's got Dave Gates with him.'

'Where are they?' Brophy asked, his usually ruddy face now like a pale pudding.

'By now, both at the back of the bank,' she said.

'I heard gunfire.'

'Yes.' Her own face was drained and now that she had brought Redwine to where he could get treatment, she felt suddenly useless. Brill sensed it.

'If you feel you're up to it, Miss Freeman, I could use some help.'

Perhaps Brophy, too, was feeling of little use for he now wandered away, purposeless, yet wanting to be useful. Presently he arrived at the same corner where Stella had stood and Brophy, too, saw the forlorn dust skimming and the dark shapes of the men up near the bank. Then down a street, opposite, he saw Gates and Orford near the corral behind the livery. Uncharacteristically, without pausing to think what he was doing, Brophy crossed Main and on his short legs went towards them. Eighty feet short of them, Orford saw him and began waving his arms to dissuade him from coming closer. 'Go on back, Mr Brophy!' Orford called. 'There's nothin' yuh can do.'

Brophy, seeming not to understand, advanced another fifty feet before stopping. He felt small and old and frustrated. It was his damn' bank and he felt he ought to be involved in some way, so he said in what he thought was a tone of authority, 'One of my employees is in there, Orford. I don't want that boy put in any more danger.'

'Some bastard has to come out an' git them horses,' said Orford stubbornly, 'an' when he does we're sure gonna nail him!'

Brophy was panting and sweating. 'No! James Fleury was shot down absolutely without mercy; and Jago's man, Mellish. The other, Culp, might not live; and now Charles Redwine's been gravely injured. No, no-one else!'

Gates said to Brophy, 'Stella Freeman heard they were already inside when your people arrived. How would they have got in?'

Brophy shook his little round head, perplexed. 'They didn't batter the doors in. They couldn't get through the window bars.'

Gates shrugged. 'Well, in there they are.'

Agitatedly, Orford said, 'Back out o' sight, quick!'

A man was behind the bank and even as Orford spoke, shot at them. Orford fired back hastily, to no result.

'Tell him to let Lanyon go and he can have the horses,' Brophy said.

But it was too late for such advice, for Orford, seeing his duty clear, was already moving, calling 'Cover me!' and heading for the horses which were now standing in relative calm, ears pricked and heads up.

Gates, now with Restall's shell-belt and long pistol slung on him, but with the army Colt still in hand, was about to give this covering fire when the man near the bank shot smokily and Orford stumbled, almost went down, then recovered and ran on, Gates blew a couple of shots away, then threw the old pistol down and drew Restall's long, oil-slick weapon with its dark hardwood butt, plain and no-nonsense like the man who had owned and preserved it.

Orford had reached the horses and, boot in stirrup, first hopping, then swinging up into the saddle, and trying to get all the horses organized, was up against the sky, exposed. It was enough to fetch the shooter at the bank into view, and when he was out Gates blasted one, the gun bucking and smoking, and the target was slapped hard, sideways, and in the space of a moment could no longer be seen by Gates.

The horses were moving away but Orford was curiously unanimated, bobbing awkwardly in the saddle, slackly, so that it did seem that he had been hit.

Brophy was aghast, seeing the denial of the horses as a bad development, and he saw himself as ultimately responsible for what might now happen to Jay Lanyon. He said urgently to Gates, 'I told him—you heard me tell him, Gates, to let them have the bloody horses...'

'It's done now,' Gates said. 'For good or ill, it's done.' Then, 'Their *remuda* man was bringing three in, so there's three men in there. I reckon I hit one.'

'Yes,' said Brophy. 'Yes, yes, and one of them has a shotgun. They say poor

Fleury was killed with it. Oh, my God, this is appalling!'

Gates said, 'Where the hell is the other way in?'

'There is none.'

Through narrowed eyes Gates watched Orford and the horses disappear among brush, their dust whirled away in the breeze. He could also see the lumpy shape of the man he had shot off the horse earlier. Then Brophy, pudgy fingers rising slowly to his face, said, 'Oh my God, the skylight!'

'What?'

'On the roof, there's a skylight.'

Pearsall, closer than Quint, actually heard Reeby get hit and called to Quint about it. 'I'll go see. Keep an eye on this shit.' And to Lanyon, 'Yuh want both barrels up your ass, try movin'.'

He found Reeby in the short passageway inside the back door, still standing, but with the side of his face pressed to the wall, his bunched fists pressed there also as though he was trying to push the wall over. Reeby's shirt had blood all over it, his face was beaded with sweat and saliva was hanging from his mouth.

When Pearsall, the shotgun in one hand, made as though to put the other on Reeby, Reeby said faintly, 'For Jesus' sake, don't touch me!' Teeth bared as in an animal snarl, gasping breaths escaping from him, pressing harder against the wall, he finally yelled as though an unseen hand had clutched at his vitals, his eyes rolled and he lost control of his bladder and slid down the wall, leaving smears of blood and urine on it. Pearsall could see that Reeby's midriff was in a mess and he could also see that in the few seconds after he had made that last great sound, Reeby had died.

'Jesus!' Pearsall spat it out in fury; but somewhere inside even this hard man there was also a chill, and for the first time he wondered if they were going to get out of this one alive, him and Quint.

Pearsall then stepped to the doorway and took a cautious look outside. No horses. No sound beyond the breeze flapping things. No-one in sight. But that meant nothing. Reeby's body lying against the wall behind him was proof enough of that.

Gates and Brophy had waited for Orford to fetch the horses around in a wide circle and finally bring them to the top end of Main. Orford had a bloody wound raked across the back of the left thigh and buttock and had been in some discomfort and sitting in blood.

Gates mounted one of the horses and they took them all to a yard and hitched them, Brophy, having declined to mount, following on his short legs.

To Orford, Gates said, 'If you can manage it you could go back an' keep 'em pinned inside that back door. I tagged one of 'em but I don't know how bad.' And then he told Orford what it was he was about to attempt now that Orford himself had been hit, and Orford, hurt as he was, his face pasty, swallowed hard and nodded. All at once he seemed to have accepted that, unable to move around with complete freedom, certainly not without pain, he could no longer strut his authority, and had come to see that, palatable or not, Gates now represented their best chance to get Lanyon out alive, for that was what Gates had said he was about to attempt.

Brophy was now most insistent that he give some help, and Gates could see that the little man would not be denied; and it suddenly came to Gates that not once had Brophy shown the slightest concern about the kind of money the bank stood to lose if those inside got away. But he said, 'I must do *something*, Mr Gates.'

He was perhaps one of the least likely men in Argon to be taking a hand in this; odd-looking, with his short legs and round body and moon face. But Gates said, 'I'd be glad of your help, Mr Brophy.'

They did tell Jago where the horses were and what was about to happen, and where Orford was, and although his pouched, hard eyes looked at Gates with undisguised dislike, he nodded curtly. 'It's mebbe the one chance we'll git.' Then, 'Listen!'

They moved nearer to the front doors of the Spanish Girl. Quint had called out and Jago answered, 'Shout it out, mister!'

'Wherever them damn' mounts is,' Quint yelled, 'I want 'em brung in! Right to this here door! When we come, we're gonna walk that boy out with us an' yuh'll hold your fire or see his haid blowed off! An' whoever it is brings them mounts comes walkin' easy, unarmed, leadin' 'em! Now git to it!'

Gates muttered something to Jago and Jago shouted, 'We hear yuh! We got to git the horses an' it's gonna take a few minutes. No harm to the boy, an' yuh'll see 'em comin' up Main right soon.'

To Brophy, Gates said, 'We'll have to move. Even so, I don't know if there's time.'

FOURTEEN

They had got a ladder out of Jago's lumber yard and had made a wide circuit so that there would be little chance of their being seen by the man at the bank who had made his loudly-shouted demands. Gates had been leading, Brophy at the other end of the ladder, trotting along like some youthful apprentice, apparently content in the belief that he was now in the thick of things.

Once they got around into the back street, from this direction they could see far off the corral livery, and a figure propped against a corner of it, Orford. When he saw them come into view, he gave them a brief hand signal.

Gates' attention, too, was fixed on the back of the bank and he was gambling that their slow, quiet approach along behind other buildings would neither be seen nor heard by anyone who might still be watching from there. Presently they went into an alley, but still well short of the bank itself.

'It'll have to be here,' Gates said. 'If we go any closer we might be seen.'

Other eyes were watching them though, from behind curtains and at black, bare panes, and some therefore saw the ladder propped against a wall in the alley and the big man, the hard-looking sodbuster, now wearing a heavy pistol, go quickly up, and once on the roof, draw the ladder up after him. Brophy went scuttling away out of sight but was not sure where he ought to go next. It was something of a let-down, for he had not wanted to quit so soon what he thought of as the scene of action.

Meantime, Jago had called up one of his bar-dogs, a sallow, pockmarked man of sad aspect, and had handed him the big Colt. 'If it all turns to shit, use it,' Jago said. He went off then, striding in a measured way out through the back door of the saloon.

Gates, up against the sky, was sliding the ladder all the way across the void of an alley, a wider one than usual, which left only a few inches of ladder on either roof; but Gates went quickly across, then had an uncertain time pulling the ladder after him. Finally he crossed a narrower gap to the roof of the bank itself and there again hauled the ladder over and laid it alongside a sturdy length of lumber which he assumed had been their means of crossing that same gap, having no doubt fetched it up through the skylight in the building behind him.

At the corner of the corral, Orford, though in mounting discomfort, watched keenly for any signs of hostile movement on the ground but now kept glancing up to where he could see Dave Gates on the roof of the bank.

Jago's pallid bar-dog, not comfortable with the unfamiliar pistol, had his attention on the front of the bank, still fervently hoping that the time would not arrive when he might have to take a hand; and he then saw the large frame of Dave Gates seeming to be walking along the sky as he made his way across one roof after another, eventually to stand on top of the Argon Bank and Loan.

The skylight itself was somewhat heavier than Gates had anticipated and its hinges were very stiff but finally he lifted the glazed flap and eased it all the way over so that it could not drop back, creating a noise, maybe at some vital time. Below him he could see that a solid-looking wooden file cabinet had been positioned beneath the opening and, not needing to fetch the ladder, he easily got down onto the top of it, then lowered himself again to stand in a dusty room—some sort of store-room—with a couple of damaged chairs in it and several other file cabinets. The floor was dirty, scraps of yellowed paper lying around, and near the toe of one of his boots, the black, wizened remains of a spent match. He crossed to the open door.

Just inside the front of the bank, Quint was bawling, 'Where's them goddamn' horses?'

No answer came, Jago's bar-dog, in his great moment, apparently tongue-tied. Then Brophy, a short distance along Main, having been sheltering in a doorway awaiting further developments, called 'A man has gone to fetch you your horses!'

'By God,' called Quint, 'if he don't git it done right soon, it's gonna be all on an' hootin'!'

Brophy then called, 'I don't know who

you are, but my name is Brophy and I am the owner of the bank; so the young man you have in there is my employee, Mr Lanyon. I ask you, sir, to release Mr Lanyon, unharmed. I am quite prepared to come into the bank in exchange. You would lose none of your bargaining-power by allowing me to do that.'

After a moment, Quint said, 'Big talk, mister. We'll sit pat with the hand we got.'

'I urge you to agree to it,' Brophy persisted.

'Open your trap ag'in,' Quint snarled, 'an' I'll *burn* your boy!'

Brophy, his face like suet, receded into his doorway.

Then Quint suddenly asked, 'Where the hell's this shave-tail lawman that's supposed to be here?'

Brophy said, 'He's been...injured.'

'Well now,' Quint said; and then, 'If them mounts ain't here in less'n one minute, I *will* start in burnin' your boy, an yuh'll know when I do because yuh'll be able to hear it, banker!'

Gates was on the stairs, going down one forward-testing step at a time, fearful that he would be heard and that if he was, they would straight away kill Jay Lanyon. He thought he could hear somebody shouting, up near the front of the bank, an exchange with someone outside. Perhaps the horses had arrived.

Pearsall was down near the still-open vault and as he came slowly down, Gates could see the back of this long-coated man who had a two-barrel shotgun in his hands. Facing the shotgunner stood Jay Lanyon, his face drained of colour, his cheeks seeming sunken, making him look older. To his eternal credit, when lifting his eyes beyond Pearsall, when he saw Gates descending, he did not react by the merest tremor of expression.

Someone out on Main called something but by the time Quint, up at the door, turned his head to look down towards Pearsall, Gates had left the stairs behind and had sunk quietly down behind one of the empty desks.

'The mounts is comin'!'

Pearsall now said to Lanyon, 'Gather up all the sacks yuh kin hold an' carry 'em up there to Quint, then come back an' git what's left. Make one move that surprises me an' it'll be the last one yuh make anywhere.'

The young man did as Pearsall had told him, walking steadily up to the front of the building, dropping the several small sacks at Quint's feet, then returned and went up a second time carrying the remainder; but he had failed to bring the cords that Reeby had put with them for lashing them onto the horses. Quint said, 'When the time comes yuh'll be the rooster that ties 'em on. Go git them cords.' Lanyon moved on back to do it.

'The cords,' he said to Pearsall, 'I forgot the cords.'

Pearsall merely grunted and called to Quint, 'How far away now?'

'Fifty yards. He's fetchin' 'em real slow. One of 'em don't want to come.'

'How many?'

'Three. We kin pack all the bags out on Reeby's.'

His mouth dry, a rhythmic hammering in his chest, while for a few moments Pearsall had been involved in this exchange, the coated man's attention distracted, Lanyon took the chance that he knew he must take if he were to clear the way for Gates; he sprang through the doorway of the vault, and solid though it was, Lanyon's was the strength of sheer terror as he pulled the steel door after him. He was now inside the still lamp-lit, narrow brick cavern, as much like a baker's oven as anything else, the steel door, at least for the moment, between him and Pearsall's shotgun. The locking device was on the outside only, and unless Lanyon's gamble paid off and Gates took a hand before it could happen, Pearsall would have this door open again soon enough.

Pearsall did indeed make his move and it was towards the door but so too did Gates take a hand by a sudden movement, going from behind one of the desks to the dubious shelter of another, and when Pearsall's staring eyes beheld the totally unexpected presence of another man inside the bank, he immediately showed his ability to react with quite amazing speed. The shotgun blasted, smoke and fragments of wad everywhere, and a wooden chair near Gates' crouching back seemed to explode into fragments.

When Gates, pistol in hand, rose from behind the desk, Pearsall, having missed his man, had retreated somewhere, probably in back of one of the wide, heavy counters. And there was now neither sight nor sound of Quint.

Gates, crouching, began going step by step towards the door of the vault, not with any notion of getting Lanyon out, for the young man was in least danger where he was, but determined that Pearsall would not get near the metal door. Yet Gates was aware of his own vulnerability now, and therefore slipped across to a position where a stout wooden cabinet stood against a wall a few feet beyond the vault; and hardly had he made this move when Pearsall, rising up from behind furniture some fourteen feet away, let go the second barrel of the shotgun with a thunderous sound inside the building, the clubbed shot striking the vault door at an angle, having passed barely a foot from Gates' head, and the myriad lead pellets went slashing off the steel with a curious tearing noise to hurtle, spreading, far and wide across the room beyond.

The noise of the gun and the rushing shot had scarcely gone before Gates was up and closing the distance between himself and Pearsall, for even if the man was carrying a pistol, his efforts to clear it away might very well be impeded by the long coat he was wearing; and if all he had was the shotgun, he would now need to reload it.

When Pearsall saw Gates coming he made a desperate effort to find cover but Gates was now shooting, the noise of the pistol assaulting his ears, the tangy smoke swirling, and Pearsall was punched first one way, then the other, as the brutal lead struck at him, and Gates himself was now on the floor, rolling, as a shot from elsewhere erupted and lead slammed the panelling of the wall behind him. Quint.

Pearsall, though grievously wounded,

was making some groping attempts to break open the shotgun, but finally, breath gasping out in short bursts, sounding like a windmill pump, Pearsall could no longer see what he was doing, then had no sense of the weight of the shotgun in his hands and he did not hear it strike the floor after it had fallen from his grasp for he was already slipping out of life towards whatever might await him elsewhere.

Gates went diving across the blood-flecked body of Pearsall, catching the foul stench of him, and so in behind one of the stoutly-built counters.

Out on Main, Jago had got the horses nearly as far as the bank when the first boom of the shotgun came, and at once he set to, releasing the common line linking all three horses, and as soon as he had done it, yelled and waved his arms to alarm the animals and send them scattering, even as the second blast of the shotgun sounded, with several explosions from Colts inside the bank. Jago was now wishing he had taken the risk of carrying a pistol, knowing that his bar-dog would never venture out across the street to fetch him one; and then he was astounded to see Brophy step out of a doorway further along Main and begin walking in his direction. Jago shouted, 'Git on back!' But Brophy, his small, round, pale face determined, as though in respect of fear, all had been done to him that could be done, and now he no longer cared.

Jago cared though, for something told him that he was in mortal danger where he was, so he backed away rapidly and at the first opportunity jogged away down an alley.

Brophy was a mere thirty feet from the bank when Quint came out, greasy-clothed, dark spiky-whiskered, sweating, his black, shallow-crowned hat hanging on thongs between his shoulders. Brophy stood as though carved out of stone as this yelling wild man, long pistol in hand, saw that the horses were not where he expected them to be, started out off the boardwalk, presumably with the intention of getting to the nearest horse when, as astonished as the bar-dog who fired, slamming lead on the brickwork of the bank behind him,

Quint hauled up fast, seeing the blue smoke bursting from under the batwing doors of the Spanish Girl.

Quint blasted one back and the checkered glass of a saloon window tinkled and flew, but he believed he would now not be able to reach the horse, so he went running along the street and down a side alley, just as Jago had done a short time before.

Gates had pulled open the door of the vault, marvelling at how Lanyon, going in, had managed to get it closed before Pearsall had been able to bring the shotgun to bear.

'There's one out on Main. Maybe by now he's got to a horse. When we're sure it's safe the best thing you can do is get right over home an' let your ma know you're not hurt.'

When they got outside, Brophy was almost at the door.

'Thank God!' Brophy said, astounding Jay Lanyon by seizing his hand and pumping it. 'Thank God!'

Gates asked, 'Where'd he go, the bastard that came out?'

'Along that alley there. Mr Jago was here. He brought their horses, then when the shooting began he scattered them, then made himself scarce.'

Lanyon took himself off across Main at a jog, heading home, but Stella Freeman appeared in the doorway of a dry goods store, the one they had taken Redwine to, so Lanyon changed direction and instead, went there.

Gates swore softly at losing the bandit who had come out on Main and, followed by Brophy, he walked back into the bank. The small canvas sacks containing the money were still stacked just inside the door.

'That's as far as it got,' said Gates. His mind was racing though, desperate to know where the last man had got to. He did not fancy some drawn-out cat-and-mouse business, with lead flying all around Argon. There were too many dead already and too many injured and a whole lot more no doubt scared shitless. And he owed it to Orford to let him know that one of them was on the loose.

Losing no more time he went through to the open back doorway, passing the fly-infested body of Reeby. Gates looked out and waved urgently to Orford who was still where he had been earlier, steadfastly covering the back, propped against corner poles of the corral.

Gates shouted, 'Take cover! One of 'em's out!'

He did not wait to see how Orford reacted but retraced his steps and this time hit the stairs at a run. Inside the top room, chest heaving from his efforts to get up there fast, he discarded spent shells and made sure the pistol was fully loaded; then he hauled himself atop the file cabinet and up through the open skylight onto the roof. Gates reasoned that from up here he stood a better chance of seeing his man, if he was still on the move, than prowling the streets, making himself a target for ambush.

The first person he saw, however, was Jago who, having obviously crossed back over Main, was now heading up towards his saloon. Jago stopped when he saw Gates rise up against the sky, then briefly raised one hand and moved on.

Gates walked all around the perimeter of the roof. The man he was looking for would want to get a saddled horse as soon as possible and now Gates actually blessed the foresight of Jago when he saw that he was assembling the loose horses at the rails outside the Spanish Girl and was securing them there. So those three horses were made safe and being covered.

Next Gates examined the nearest livery and corral and saw that Orford had moved across to the far side and was kneeling, observing between the poles. He did see Gates though, and made a quick hand signal.

Gates went to the far side of the roof, trying to see the other Argon livery, to spot anyone moving near it, or in fact to catch sight of any horses anywhere that might prove to be a magnet.

The eruptions of gunfire at the bank had certainly had the effect of deterring all those within earshot who might have thought to venture outside. Argon was like a graveyard, the little breeze lifting from time to time, the dust skimming and a few tumbleweeds bowling along, a somewhat sad and spiritless sight, Gates thought.

The first that Orford knew of the man's presence was when there was the loud sound of a pistol, and bark and dust flew from one of the corral poles, provoking the several penned horses to a minor panic.

Orford swung around, firing, but saw only the flick of dark movement as the shooter withdrew around the corner of the livery building. Orford went through between the poles, his thigh and buttock hurting as though a hot poker had been laid across them, but he pressed on, in and out between the unsettled horses until he emerged on the opposite side of the corral, where he had been earlier.

When he heard the Colt go off, Gates felt a sense of trembling shock and the first image that flashed into his mind was one, not of Argon, but of Laramie, and of Luke Jensen dying there in a place that ought to have been safe; that Gates had told him was safe; and now Gates had exchanged a wave with another young lawman, had had the advantage of an elevated place, a much better chance of seeing imminent danger but had sighted none and moved away. *Sighted none. Missed something.* He was going across the roof at a shambling run, still hearing voices from another time. *'Garvey's down! Go left! Go left! The barn's cleared!'*

At the edge of the roof he felt an almighty flood of relief when he saw Orford, pistol in hand—though in the act of working his way along the nearside of the corral—apparently no more hurt than he had been a few minutes earlier. Orford was not looking in his direction.

Gates' relief was at once dampened, however, when he saw a big, darkly-dressed man, hat hanging between his shoulder blades, moving quietly along the back of the livery, then going to ground near a plump rain-barrel, clearly having seen Orford and waiting for him to come into full view at the corner of the corral.

Gates yelled. Orford stopped as though

suddenly paralyzed. Quint, rising, saw the elevated figure of Gates and let fly with a racketing shot amid gunsmoke, the lead actually flicking Gates' left sleeve; and Gates, marvelling at such shooting, banged one away also, and missed, and then another very fast, as Quint had begun coming forward to close on Orford, and that one got him, made him drop his head as he was spun against the corral. But then like some wild beast that has been wounded, Quint let go another shot, this time through the corral, sending wood-bark flying and missing Orford by a whisker. Then Quint had got himself behind the water-cask again, perhaps reloading.

Urgently Gates was waving Orford away, wanting him to lengthen the range as far as possible, but as Orford acknowledged him it became instantly clear that he could move only stiffly, almost dragging one leg, and in alarm Gates now saw Quint, blood on him, but like an enraged bull, coming away from the livery at an awkward jog, intent on closing in on Orford to kill him, and evidently careless of Gates' presence on the roof.

As Quint's arm came up, Gates shot, and Quint, as though hit with a spade, staggered back and to the side; yet unbelievably he began to come on again, weaving a little but with his attention utterly fixed on the hobbling Orford.

Gates, his pistol arm extended, standing quite still against the sky, shot him. A spray of blood went flying from Quint as his head was snapped back and he was flung down to lie on his back, dust rising.

Orford had managed to turn round but the pistol had fallen from his hand and he was utterly spent, kneeling then, vomiting, and it was the sour bile of fear.

Gates stood with Restall's pistol now hanging by his side, his chest rising and falling as though he had been running to near-exhaustion.

The attempt on the bank at Argon was over.

FIFTEEN

During the time he had been under the menace of the men who had come into Argon, Jay Lanyon one by one had heard their names: Quint, Pearsall, Reeby, Sears.

Now those same men were all gone into the dry earth, their narrow places marked simply with those unadorned, unqualified names; and not far from these four lay James Fleury whose similarly unlikely neighbours in death were Mellish and Culp, who indeed as Doc Brill had feared, had not survived the combined hazards of loss of blood and the trauma of his fearsome wound.

Charles Redwine had survived, however, though Brill considered that the attorney's left shoulder and his left arm movements were likely to be somewhat impaired; and it would be some while before Redwine would next attempt the steep ascent to his office. The Argon sheriff, Matt Orford, another survivor, was today moving around with less discomfort but he knew how close he had come to suffering the same fate as Culp.

So Redwine was not to be seen, but it did appear that nearly everybody else had turned out for the burials and were now still standing around much as they had done after the burying of George Restall as if, for some unapparent reason, they were reluctant to leave.

The once anonymous bar-dog from Jago's Spanish Girl saloon whose name turned out to be Pask and who, by one well-timed—some had gone as far as to say crucial—shot at Quint, when that fearsome man had been trying to get to a horse, had ensured himself a place in the lore of Argon, now also found himself being spoken to agreeably by more people in the town than previously would have even known of his existence. Brophy, no less, clouded in cigar smoke, had pumped Pask's hand twice.

These were minor indications, perhaps

quite early manifestations of a different outlook beginning to be seen among a community that in recent days had been badly shaken, yet it was too early to say whether or not these new attitudes would endure. Suffice to say that for the present they were visible.

The behaviour of those who had turned out to sing the hymns and join in the murmuring of prayers, fell into two distinct styles, even though all of the people had been and were, intermingling; one group, by far the larger, a subdued one, consisting of all those citizens who had taken no active part in the resistance to the raid on the Argon Bank and Loan (though now that it was all safely over, most of them probably wished that they had), and a much smaller number consisting of those who had taken part, one way or another: Jago, his pockmarked bar-dog, Doc Brill, Pauling (perhaps the least likely of all, a man who had by no means sat on the fence), Charles Redwine *(in absentia)*, Brophy, Jay Lanyon, Sheriff Orford (being so referred to and with some frequency by all and sundry) and to whom had been made a presentation of a worn silver watch found on the body of one of the bandits, Stella Freeman and, of course, Gates.

And some who had been in the action, even if only on the fringe,—like Pauling and Pask—were seen to be adopting a quite similar calm, even studiedly offhand manner, having not only taken part in a highly dangerous affair, but having emerged relatively unscathed to stand before their fellows.

Pask, indeed, having grown in confidence, was now examining with unconcealed interest those who were moving around slowly in the crowd, joining this group and that, until even Pask could perceive that after a time, as by some natural interaction, those who had stood out from the common herd on that violent morning, eventually tended to find like company, or to stand apart from the rest. Jago was perhaps the exception, being in earnest conversation with the black-haired, pretty woman, Millie Porter. Lanyon was standing alongside his employer, Brophy.

Pauling, usually to be seen with Ed Moore, today was not, but had joined Sheriff Orford, and even seemed to be dominating the conversation. Doc Brill had just now moved cross to speak to Jago; and Dave Gates who, from time to time, everybody had paused to look at, was in what seemed to be a serious discussion with the schoolteacher, Stella Freeman. Whatever they were talking about, Pask of course could not tell, for they were some little distance from him, but he did see them eventually go strolling away along Main, still much engrossed in whatever it was. Pask saw Jago remove his cigar for a moment and watch them too, until the Porter woman said something and she and Jago laughed and he gave her a light slap on the hip and then they, too, wandered away, heading off towards the edge of the town, where Millie Porter's house stood.

Little by little the groups, too, began breaking up, the crowd dispersing.

When, after maybe ten minutes, few people were to be seen, Pask also made his hands-in-pockets way back towards the Spanish Girl.

The Lanyons had gone home, and Pauling, Doc Brill and Brophy, and an almost weird calm had settled upon the town. A small breeze was lightly skimming the yellow dust, a dog was sniffing absently along a boardwalk, and Orford, the Argon peacemaker, his new hat looking as though it had been hard-used in recent times, and with only the smallest evidence of stiffness in his walk, came pacing easily along, alone. Anyone seeing him from a distance who had not lately been to this place, and were too far off to distinguish his youthful cast of features, might well have mistaken him, by that easy, unspectacular gait, one that held no hint of swagger, for another peacekeeper once well known and much respected around these same streets of Argon.

This Large Print Book for the Partially sighted, who cannot read normal print, is published under the auspices of

THE ULVERSCROFT FOUNDATION

THE ULVERSCROFT FOUNDATION

. . . we hope that you have enjoyed this Large Print Book. Please think for a moment about those people who have worse eyesight problems than you . . . and are unable to even read or enjoy Large Print, without great difficulty.

You can help them by sending a donation, large or small to:

**The Ulverscroft Foundation,
1, The Green, Bradgate Road,
Anstey, Leicestershire, LE7 7FU,
England.**

or request a copy of our brochure for more details.

The Foundation will use all your help to assist those people who are handicapped by various sight problems and need special attention.

Thank you very much for your help.

Other DALES Western Titles In Large Print

ELLIOT CONWAY
The Dude

JOHN KILGORE
Man From Cherokee Strip

J. T. EDSON
Buffalo Are Coming

ELLIOT LONG
Savage Land

HAL MORGAN
The Ghost Of Windy Ridge

NELSON NYE
Saddle Bow Slim